**'What's the matter?'** He must have sensed her reaction because the dark head raised and she looked into glittering eyes.

'Relax, damn it. I'm not about to take you in the back of a taxi.'

How dared he? She sat upright with a sharp jerk, her face blazing. 'Believe me, Carter, you wouldn't get the chance,' she bit out furiously. 'I don't know what sort of woman you're used to wining and dining, but it would take more than a good meal and a bottle of wine to get me into bed.'

'Really?' He looked amused and unperturbed by her rage, folding his arms and surveying her with expressionless eyes. 'What would it take, then?'

'More than you've got,' she shot back nastily.

'Is that a challenge?' he asked silkily.

**Helen Brooks** lives in Northamptonshire and is married with three children. As she is a committed Christian, busy housewife and mother, her spare time is at a premium, but her hobbies include reading, swimming, gardening and walking her two energetic, inquisitive and very endearing young dogs. Her long-cherished aspiration to write became a reality when she put pen to paper on reaching the age of forty, and sent the result off to Mills & Boon®.

**Recent titles by the same author:**

MISTRESS BY AGREEMENT
THE CHRISTMAS MARRIAGE MISSION
THE PASSIONATE HUSBAND

# HIS MARRIAGE ULTIMATUM

BY
HELEN BROOKS

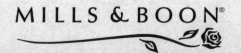

MILLS & BOON®

*MILLS & BOON and MILLS & BOON with the Rose Device are registered trademarks of the publisher.*

*First published in Great Britain 2004*
*Paperback edition 2005*
*Harlequin Mills & Boon Limited,*
*Eton House, 18-24 Paradise Road, Richmond, Surrey TW9 1SR*

© Helen Brooks 2004

ISBN 0 263 84112 X

*Set in Times Roman 10½ on 12 pt.*
*01-0105-53872*

*Printed and bound in Spain*
*by Litografía Rosés, S.A., Barcelona*

# CHAPTER ONE

'I JUST can't believe you had that gorgeous man eating out of your hand and then you send him packing. If there was any justice in this world he'd at least have come to me for a shoulder to cry on, poor lamb.'

'Can we have a reality check here?' Liberty Fox surveyed her mother through half-closed eyes, her voice mocking as she lounged back against the cream leather sofa in the ultra-modern room. She knew the tone and lack of heated response would annoy the older woman, which was exactly why she was curbing her inner resentment. 'Gerard Bousquet is no poor lamb, Mother. I caught him cheating on me and I finished our relationship. End of story.'

'But you said he arrived on your doorstep with flowers and chocolate, suitably penitent and promising he'd never stray again. You might at least have given him one more chance. He was *so* handsome.'

Liberty kept the nonchalant pose a moment longer before she straightened, reaching for the cup of coffee in front of her as she said coolly, 'Handsome is as handsome does.'

'There you see; that's exactly what I mean about you.' Miranda Walker wriggled delicate shoulders gracefully. 'I've never understood what you say any more than I understand you. Handsome is as handsome does! What does that mean, for goodness' sake?'

'It means that Gerard is history,' Liberty said dryly,

taking a sip of coffee before she added, 'fidelity is an absolute with me, Mother. Not an option.'

The shoulders moved again. 'You're so pedantic, Liberty. Just like your father.'

Don't bite; that's what she wants you to do, Liberty warned herself, taking another sip of the excellent coffee—her mother only had the best—to quell the hot words hovering on her tongue. If all else failed, her mother knew she could catch her on the raw when she talked about her first husband—Liberty's father—in that scathing tone. She breathed deeply before she said, keeping her voice even, 'Being compared to Dad is all right with me, Mother.'

'I don't doubt it.' There was more than a touch of petulance in Miranda's voice when she said, 'It would be a different story if it was me, of course.'

She really didn't want to do this today, not with her feelings still so raw after Gerard's betrayal. It was one thing to present the situation to her mother in a slightly offhand, almost amused manner—quite another to face the fact that Gerard had been seeing someone else whilst declaring undying love to her. Liberty uncrossed and crossed her legs, finishing her coffee and unwrapping the slender foil-covered chocolate cream in the saucer. If ever she needed the comfort of chocolate it was now. The diet could wait.

She relished the luxurious silky feel of the confectionery on her tongue before she said, 'We're not alike, Mother. We never have been.'

'Quite.'

There was a charged silence before Liberty raised her eyes and took in the ethereal, amazingly youthful-looking figure staring at her with unconcealed annoyance. Miranda didn't look a day over thirty—in spite of approaching her half-century milestone in a few months. Cosmetic surgery and a positively paranoid desire to be a female Peter Pan had ensured her mother had the face and figure many an ageing film star would have killed for. Three hours at the gym every day, no red meat, no puddings, no alcohol— Liberty had grown up with her mother's bible on life, and there was no doubt the small blonde woman looking at her now with open hostility could turn any man's head.

Finely boned, with porcelain skin, natural blonde hair and deep blue eyes set in a face which was truly heart-shaped—Miranda had it all. She had also had five husbands to date and was in the middle of a particularly acrimonious divorce from the last one, who objected to his wife's demand for half his fortune. Liberty found it surprising that he hadn't expected something like this, considering her mother had got richer and richer with each succeeding marriage. She had left her first husband— Liberty's father—for a wealthy financier and hadn't looked back since.

'I have to be going.' Liberty rose to her feet, her shoes sinking in the ankle-deep carpet which always made her feel as though she was wading through mud. Her mother had been thrilled with the fabulously expensive chrome and glass apartment overlooking the Thames when she had married her fifth husband six years before, but Liberty felt it resembled a goldfish bowl. A lavish, extravagant and inordinately high-priced goldfish bowl admittedly, but a goldfish bowl nevertheless. 'I have an appointment at two o'clock.'

Miranda wrinkled her small nose. 'One of your awful cases, I suppose?'

'It's business, yes.' Her mother had never understood why she had determined to be a solicitor rather than catching herself a wealthy husband and living a life of ease.

'And what shall I say to Gerard if I happen to run into

him?' Miranda asked peevishly. 'You do remember it was at one of *my* dinner parties you first met him?'

That should have told her something. It was the first time she had ever dated one of the people from her mother's circle, and it would certainly be the last. 'Ask him how—' Liberty frowned as though she couldn't remember the name, the frown clearing as she said '—how Alexia Lemaire is. Okay? And if he has any difficulty remembering the name, remind him it's the female who was in bed with him when I called round his apartment unexpectedly.'

Miranda sniffed eloquently. 'These things happen with hot-blooded men like Gerard; they don't mean anything.'

Not to her mother maybe, but then Miranda had been the 'other woman' so often that unfaithfulness was a word which just didn't register in her vocabulary. 'Goodbye, Mother.' Liberty walked to the door after bending forward and touching each scented cheek with her lips, the only embrace her mother allowed. 'I'll talk to you soon.'

Once out in the crisp October afternoon Liberty paused for a moment, taking great deep breaths of the city-laden air. It carried myriad traffic fumes in its depths but it was still preferable to her mother's overheated, scented surroundings.

She felt better once she was seated in her little Ford Ka, but only slightly. A visit to her mother's always resulted in a sick feeling in the pit of her stomach and a host of emotions and memories tumbling about her head. She sat for a moment with her hands resting on the leather-clad steering wheel, willing herself to calm down. Even this car—a thirtieth birthday present to herself six months before—had caused an argument with her mother. Miranda hadn't been able to understand why she hadn't gone for a sporty little number or a racy coupé, and Liberty's explanation that she wanted a sweet-driving small car which looked good and was talented enough to take her anywhere had been lost on her mother.

Liberty patted the pale grey fascia. 'I love you anyway,' she said out loud, her thoughts still on the expensively dressed and *coiffured* woman in the fabulous apartment she had just left as she pulled out into the lunchtime traffic.

A squeal of brakes culminating in an impact which rattled her teeth informed her of her mistake even before her brain registered she hadn't checked her mirrors.

She sat quite still, shock causing her to freeze for long seconds before she forced her numb mind and body into action. As she opened her door she saw the driver of the other car—who had slewed across the road in an effort to avoid her—exiting his vehicle, a prestige, state-of-the-art Mercedes in gleaming slate-blue. He reached her just as she stood shakily to her feet.

'Are you all right?' he asked very evenly.

A pair of granite-grey eyes held hers, and in the time it took for her to realise the man wasn't as old as she had thought at first, and that the streaks of grey in the jet-black hair had misled her, she felt her knees start to buckle.

She heard him swear softly as he grabbed her, holding her against him as he said, 'Breathe deeply a few times,' whilst he opened her car door again, positioning her sideways in the seat with her feet on the road. She felt her head being pushed down to her knees but couldn't resist, the all-consuming faintness rendering her helpless.

How long she remained like that she was never very sure, but it could only have been a matter of some sixty seconds or so before the dizzy weakness began to clear. 'I'm sorry.'

She was aware of him standing next to her and the sound of car horns in the background, but all he said was,

'Take your time,' as though they weren't blocking a major road at the height of the midday rush hour.

'I...I'll back in again, shall I?' As she recovered her voice along with her senses she tried to get a grasp on the situation. 'Maybe you could park somewhere close and we'll exchange numbers and so on?' she suggested more briskly.

'Do you feel able to drive?'

She raised her head and looked him fully in the face for the first time. He had a lovely voice, very deep and almost gravelly but with a dark smokiness which took away any roughness. The sort of voice which would have made him a wow on the silver screen. He was attractive, too, in a somewhat unorthodox kind of way, his face too strong and tough for straightforward handsomeness but carrying a quality which was more powerful than pretty-boy good looks. She pulled herself together fast as she realised he was waiting for an answer to his question. 'Yes, yes of course,' she said hastily. 'I'm only going to back into the parking space I've just left.'

He said nothing more, but the raising of black eyebrows a fraction and the expression on the hard-planed face made it very clear exactly what he thought of her driving prowess.

The colour was hot in her cheeks as she watched him walk over to his car, but then she shrugged mentally as she concentrated on backing into the neat little space she had vacated so arbitrarily just minutes before. She couldn't blame him if he was less than enamoured with her performance to date; the accident had been totally her fault. Why hadn't she checked her mirrors? She groaned inwardly. Basic procedure, something you did without thinking. Only she hadn't.

Once she had parked she nerved herself to get out of

the car and inspect the damage. Although he had obviously swerved violently and avoided going headlong into the side of her, the glancing blow to the rear had all but taken off the bumper, smashed the back light and dented the side bodywork. It was a mess.

A horrifying urge to burst into tears brought Liberty's back straightening and her chin lifting. He already thought she was a menace to all road users; she wasn't about to compound the image by giving way to waterworks.

She reached for her handbag on the passenger seat and hunted through for her insurance details, only to give another inward groan as she realised they were in the bag she had used the day before. She always made sure she was fully coordinated down to the smallest detail when visiting her mother, and the black bag of the day before hadn't lent itself to the french-navy suit she was wearing today. Great. She swallowed hard. This was turning into one swell day.

She raised her head, glancing along the pavement as a tall commanding figure, who looked to be at least three or four inches taller than anyone else in the vicinity, caught her attention. It was him. Of course, it had to be—it went with the afternoon.

She watched him striding easily towards her with the sort of nonchalant arrogance which said his handle on life was very secure. He wasn't hurrying but his long legs seemed to cover the distance between them before she could blink. He had a fantastic body.

The thought, coming from nowhere as it did, shocked her into lowering her eyes, and she rummaged in her bag as he drew alongside, pretending to still look for her papers.

'Problem?'

'I'm afraid so.' She was ready this time when she looked

at him and didn't allow the flinty gaze to make an impact. 'It seems I've left my insurance details in my other bag.'

He nodded.

It wasn't a very nice nod, she thought irritably. It was a nod which said he might have expected something like this, or was she just being paranoid? 'I can give you my name and address and registration number and so on,' she said quickly, aware she was babbling but unable to help herself. 'And I'm fully aware everything was my fault. Is…is your car badly damaged?'

'No.' He didn't elaborate, looking down at her with a narrowed, assessing stare before he said, 'Don't you know it's foolish to accept liability?'

She couldn't hide the annoyance now, her voice something of a snap when she said, 'I don't play games, Mr—?'

'Blake. Carter Blake.'

'I don't play games, Mr Blake. The accident was my fault and I'm just glad no one was injured. I'm fully prepared to take responsibility for my mistake.'

A brief smile touched his lips and then disappeared. 'Unusual attribute in this day and age,' he drawled smoothly, quite unmoved by her antagonism.

She couldn't agree more. Her work highlighted this all too sad fact every day. However, for some reason this man had got well and truly under her skin and it went against the grain to see eye to eye with him about anything. She'd also just realised the pen she kept in her handbag—an expensive if showy gold one her mother had bought her for Christmas some years before, but which would have been ideal for suggesting she was a woman of substance to this smug individual—was nestled with the insurance papers and other bits and pieces in the bag at home. She had been in a rush that morning, having overslept due to some pills she'd taken last thing the night before for a persistent headache, and had just grabbed keys, purse, phone and lipstick before leaving the house. Stupid, stupid, stupid.

'Do you have a name?'

She was brought out of her whirling self-censure as he extended a hand, a very large hand, towards her. 'Liberty Fox,' she managed a little breathlessly as she placed her fingers in his, the feel of his warm, firm flesh disconcerting to say the least.

'How do you do.' He didn't prolong the contact, for which she was grateful. Something akin to mild electric shocks had radiated through her nerves. 'Let me give you my card, Liberty.' He reached into the breast pocket of the dark charcoal suit jacket he was wearing—a jacket which sat perfectly on shoulders broad enough to belong to a professional wrestler—and brought out a small business card. 'Why don't you ring me later when we both have more time?' he suggested silkily.

'But—' she stopped abruptly, not knowing how to put it.

The black eyebrows rose. 'Yes?'

'Don't you want my telephone number, an address, car details? Something?'

Firm lips twitched. 'You've already informed me you are prepared to take responsibility for this incident,' he said reasonably.

'But you don't know me.' She stared at him militantly. 'I might be lying. I might be the sort of person who will make sure you never see or hear from me again.'

'I don't think so,' he murmured, studying her with cool amusement. He had thought at first she was very average-looking, nothing special, but he had been wrong. In spite of trying to be severe and assertive, the soft, full mouth

and anxious brown eyes spoke of the real woman behind
the image the executive suit and stern hairstyle projected.
How long was her hair? His eyes moved to the tightly
restrained, thick coil at the back of her head. No way of
knowing. But the colour was wonderful, a true russet. He'd
read somewhere that the word came from a kind of rough-
skinned, reddish-brown apple, but her skin was like pure
peaches and cream. It would feel velvety and silky-smooth
to the touch, each rounded curve…

The sudden stirring his body gave surprised him and he
cut off the train of thought with a ruthlessness which was
habitual. It had been a long time since he had felt such a
strong sexual attraction for a woman he didn't know, and
he wasn't altogether comfortable with it. He preferred his
relationships to be fully under his control from beginning
to end. At thirty-six years of age he was long past the stage
of blind desire.

He took a physical step backwards as he said, 'I tell you
what, prove or disprove my gut feeling about you. Okay?
If you don't ring I'll put it down to experience and no hard
feelings. But I'm already late for an important appointment
and I have to go.'

'Oh, right.' He had taken her aback and she realised it
was obvious from the slight smile touching the corners of
his mouth. She hated the satisfaction it undoubtedly gave
him as much as she objected to the mocking expression in
his eyes. It would serve him right if she *didn't* ring, she
told herself angrily, her lips closing into a tight line. He
clearly expected the whole human race to dance to his
tune. One or two of her mother's husbands had been men
of the same ilk, and she had often thanked God her own
father was different.

'That's settled then.' He smiled, a confident, I-don't-care-what-you-do smile that caused every muscle in her body to clench. 'Goodbye, Miss Fox.'

Miss Fox? Where had the Liberty gone? She was so busy dwelling on that she didn't realise until much later he must have taken the trouble to look at her hand to determine the absence of a wedding ring. 'Goodbye,' she said hastily as he began to turn away. 'And thank you for being so reasonable,' she called somewhat belatedly as he strode away.

'Reasonable is my second name.' It was tossed over his shoulder and he didn't turn his head; nevertheless she could tell he was smiling again by the tone of his voice.

She had been a source of constant amusement to the man, she thought irritably, before immediately feeling a pang of conscience. Most people in his position would have been extremely irate to say the least, if not downright hostile. He had been courteous and pleasant despite the fact she had caused the accident which had now delayed him for some important appointment or other.

So why had she felt such immediate antipathy towards him? she asked herself, climbing back into the car and relaxing in the driver's seat with a small sigh as she shut her eyes for a moment. She wasn't normally like this. She prided herself on the fact that she could get on with anyone. Well, anyone except her mother, she qualified silently.

As her mobile phone began to ring she forced herself out of the reverie, reaching for her bag and checking who it was before she answered. Dad! If there was one person in all the world she wanted to speak to right now, it was her father. He had always been her mainstay; her anchor and comforter when she was young and her best friend and bulwark as she had grown.

Despite being a single parent when Miranda had left them both for the financier when Liberty was just three years old, he had juggled a demanding job as a GP with being mother and father to a small toddler who had been thrown utterly at sea by her mother's desertion. And never once had he indicated by word or action that she was a burden or that having her around curtailed his chances of meeting someone else. He had always been there for her, always sensing if she needed him.

'Dad?' She found she was biting back the tears as she spoke into the phone.

'Hi, Pumpkin.' The familiar voice was balm to her soul. 'Fancy eating with the old man tonight?'

'Tonight?' She was surprised. They always had Sunday lunch together, cooked by her father's housekeeper, Mrs Harris—a grim-looking individual with a heart of gold who had done her own share of bringing Liberty up—but today was Thursday. 'I'd love to,' she responded after an infinitesimal pause. 'I've just bumped the car so seeing you would be a perfect pick-me-up.'

'Are you all right?'

The concern in his voice warmed her heart but made the tears begin to prick the back of her eyes again, and she had to clear her throat before she could say, 'I'm fine, Dad, really. It was my fault. I didn't check my mirror and caused some poor guy to clip my rear but he was very good about it. I'd just called to see Mother.'

'Ah.'

He didn't need to say anything else; her father knew better than anyone how such meetings affected her equilibrium.

'What time do you want me at the house?' she asked, forcing a bright note into her voice so he would know she really was okay.

There was the briefest of pauses and then he said quietly, 'I wasn't planning to eat at home tonight. The thing is, I'd like you to meet someone and I thought a slap-up meal somewhere might be nice.'

Liberty held the phone away from her ear and stared at it for a second. In spite of the quietness of his voice there had been an underlying excitement there too. 'Someone?' she asked carefully as she placed the instrument back to her face.

'An old friend. No, not really an old friend.' Another pause, longer this time. 'I don't know if you remember Joan Andrews. She worked at the practice for a time when you were about seven or eight.'

'Yes, I remember Joan.' She had been the practice nurse, a small, homely body with apple-red cheeks and a wide smile. Liberty seemed to recall Joan and her husband had emigrated to Australia or New Zealand, she couldn't remember which. 'I thought she lived abroad?'

'She did. They did, her husband and Joan. The thing is…'

As his voice trailed away again, Liberty's heart began to race slightly. He'd said 'the thing is' twice in the space of a minute; something was afoot. What was the thing? She asked just that but her father didn't reply to this directly. Instead he said, 'Joan's husband was an alcoholic; that was one of the reasons they emigrated. He had a brother out there who owned a large farm and was prepared to take Joan's husband on as manager. She was hoping it would be enough for him to give up the drink.'

'Was it?' She wasn't quite sure why they were discussing Joan's husband.

'For a time, then he started drinking worse than ever. She stayed with him till the end. It was his liver that finally gave out.'

'Right.' She waited for the rest of it.

'We fell in love, Liberty, all those years ago. Hard to

believe more than two decades have passed. We never did anything about it, of course—she had her husband and she wouldn't have abandoned him, it'd have been the death of him, and I—'

This time she spoke into the pause. 'You had me to look after,' she said softly.

'You weren't an issue; Joan adored you,' he said quickly. 'She couldn't have kids of her own; her husband had a motorbike accident just after they were married and the result was that all that side of their marriage was null and void. That's what started him drinking apparently, poor devil.'

Liberty found she didn't know what to say. She'd had no idea her father had ever felt that way about Joan or Joan about him, but then she had been a mere child at the time. She tried to keep her voice normal when she said, 'When did you meet her again?'

'Two days ago. She just walked into the surgery.' The lilt in his voice was back. 'Her husband died three months ago and she's been busy putting her affairs in order but now she's back in England for good. She said she was making contact with old friends but as soon as we saw each other again we knew we felt the same. Absence really had made the heart grow fonder.'

She could hardly take it in. Her father carrying a secret love in his heart all these years? But it explained a lot. He was a very handsome man with the added allure of being a doctor; she had seen women making goo goo eyes at him over the years. But he'd never been interested and now she knew why. Joan Andrews. She shook her head slowly in amazement.

'I'm glad for you, Dad.' And she was, she really was, in spite of the selfish little pang her heart had given at the knowledge that she wouldn't be the number one person in his life any longer.

'You'll come and meet her again tonight then?'

'Of course I will, I'd love to,' she lied enthusiastically. The truth of the matter was that she would have liked twenty-four hours to get used to the fact that her father had turned into a couple overnight.

'Great. Joan'll be thrilled. I think she was a bit worried you might feel she was taking me away from you.'

He laughed with the insensitivity of a father who thought his daughter was perfect and could never have a self-centred thought in her life, and Liberty responded with an appropriate laugh of her own before she said, 'It's high time you had someone to share your life with and from the sound of it she's had no picnic up to yet.' And she meant every word.

'Thanks, Pumpkin.' Her father's voice was husky now, and there was a brief silence before he said, 'Eight o'clock at the Phoenix suit you?'

'The Phoenix?' This really was true love. It cost an arm and a leg for so much as a glass of wine at the Phoenix, one of London's most exclusive nightclubs. Liberty had only been there once before when a date had been hoping to impress her. The man in question had been hoping for a lot more too—courtesy of payment for her dinner—and had been more than a little offended when she had rebuffed his arrogant advances and compounded what he saw as an insult to his male prowess when she had sent a cheque for the cost of her dinner to him the next day. 'Best bib and tucker then?' she teased lightly.

'You bet.' Her father chuckled like an excited school-boy. 'See you later. I'll be watching out for you. And…thanks again, Pumpkin,' he added softly.

This was turning into one crazy day. She sat for a full

minute more mulling over all her father had said before she started the engine, but on the drive back to the office it wasn't her father and Joan Andrews who filled her mind, but a tall, broad, tough-looking individual with eyes the colour of a stormy winter sky. And she knew she was going to ring Carter Blake's number.

## CHAPTER TWO

LIBERTY told herself she shouldn't have been surprised when the rest of the afternoon turned into a maniac merry-go-round, mainly due to an extensive power cut just after she returned from lunch. One of her father's favourite sayings was that it never rained but it poured, and with all the practice computers rendered helpless and irate clients at every turn, the day just got worse and worse.

By six o'clock she felt a frazzled wreck, and if it had been anyone else but her father she was seeing that night she would have rung and made her excuses, the thought of a long hot bath and an early night taking on the appearance of heaven.

She was one of the last to leave the offices in Finsbury, east London, but that wasn't unusual. She was aiming to become a junior partner within the next five years, and that wouldn't happen without dedication and hard work. Normally she caught the tube to and from work, but owing to her lunch date with her mother she had decided to use the car that morning. As she stood and stared at it in the practice car park, she reflected that it hadn't been one of her better decisions.

But she couldn't think about booking the car into a garage just now. She had the evening to get through and then a long day in front of her tomorrow; the car could wait.

She drove home very carefully, conscious that she was tired and that another accident was the last thing she needed. Her mood lifted as she drew into the tree-lined street in Whitechapel where she had recently bought her first home. After leaving law college, she had spent two years serving articles with her present firm whilst still living at home with her father, but once she had been offered a permanent position had felt the time was right to leave the nest for a rented bedsit. Another rented property, this time a one-bedroomed flat, had followed three years later, but at the beginning of the year she had come across the small, one-bed seventeenth-century almshouse—originally built for 'decay'd' seamen or their widows, according to the estate-agent blurb—being advertised in the local paper. She had felt good about the house even then.

The ground floor consisted of a living room and bedroom, with a kitchen, dining room and separate bathroom in the basement and a Lilliputian garden at the rear just big enough to hold a garden table and two chairs and a selection of flowering potted shrubs grouped round a stone bird table and bird-bath.

The lady owner had been retiring and moving to live with a sister in Cornwall after twenty-five years in the house and, against all the advice she would have offered someone else, Liberty had immediately declared herself to be in love with the place and offered the full asking price. She had been installed in her quaint little home within the month, complete with a hefty mortgage which meant she would have to tighten her belt for the forseeable future.

But it was worth it. As she exited the car a shaft of cold autumn sunlight caught the tiny panes in the living room window, causing them to twinkle and glow. Oh yes, it was worth it all right, she thought, mounting the eight walled steps leading up to the stout front door with renewed vigour. She was autonomous, self-sufficient and self-supporting and she would never, *ever* be beholden to any man to get her the things she wanted.

Liberty did not consciously think of her mother at this

point, but the woman who had had such an adverse effect on her personality and her life was under the surface of her mind nevertheless.

The front door opened straight into the living room, which was warm and cosy and comforting. After kicking off her shoes, Liberty flung herself down onto one of her two plump two-seater sofas, which were covered in a vibrant shade of terracotta. She stretched before relaxing her limbs, eyes shut. She loved this room. The oyster curtains and carpet which she'd bought along with the house had been a perfect backdrop for the sofas she had acquired a year or so before seeing her home, and the bookcase behind her and old original fireplace gave a permanence to the surroundings which was wonderfully cheering.

But somehow, tonight, the usual magic wasn't working. She sat up, frowning slightly. Carter Blake. The wretched man was demanding her attention as he had all through the long afternoon. She might just as well phone him now.

She reached for her handbag and extracted the card. She had glanced at it earlier, expecting a formal business card or something of that nature, but instead there had just been his name with a couple of numbers, one designated as a mobile. Was the other his home? She stared at it, the frown deepening as she resolutely ignored the quickening of her heartbeat.

She would phone him and, if he didn't answer, leave a message before she began to get ready. She glanced at her watch. She'd order a taxi for tonight first though.

The taxi booked, she felt both annoyed and perplexed with herself when she realised her heart was thudding like crazy at the thought of making the second telephone call. 'Get a grip, Libby.' She spoke out loud into the quietness. 'He's just a man. Two arms, two legs and no doubt a very inflated opinion of himself.' The last few years in the market-place of life had shown her that men like Carter Blake—attractive, forceful men who wore arrogance like a second skin—*always* had an inflated opinion of themselves!

She made a face. That being the case, she wouldn't rush to phone him after all. She would leave it for a day or two, or at least until tomorrow. She barely had time to shower and get ready for her father's big night as it was.

By the time the taxi hooted its arrival outside, Liberty had bathed, creamed and *coiffured* herself into quite a different creature from the smart and rigidly formal Miss Fox of daytime hours. She rarely let her hair down—both metaphorically and literally—but, ever since a pair of granite-grey eyes had given her a cool once-over, a spirit of rebellion seemed to have taken hold. And the Phoenix *did* require something that bit special.

Her normally sedate hair was now framing a fully made-up face in a silky shoulder-length bob, the classic black evening dress she was wearing giving the illusion of restraint until one noticed the thigh-length slits either side of the pencil-slim skirt. Gerard had urged her to buy the dress for a forthcoming dinner-dance they had been supposed to attend before his liaison with the kittenish Alexia, and she was glad now she had insisted on paying for it herself. It would have been a shame to get rid of such a gorgeous gown but she would have if he had contributed so much as a penny towards it.

There was a lump in her throat as she checked her reflection one last time as the taxi hooted again. And then she swallowed it away, her brown eyes darkening to ebony as she lifted her chin. Gerard wasn't worth one tear. He was a liar and a cheat and she was well rid of him.

Once in the taxi she pulled her coat more closely around her and tried to ignore the fact that everyone outside the window seemed to be in twos. It must have rained a little while she was getting ready because the pavements were glistening and wet, circles of muted gold here and there where the street lights banished the darkness.

She'd been so stupid to let Gerard Bousquet become more than a casual acquaintance, to let him persuade her that she didn't have to be alone in the years ahead and that she could share her life with someone else. Although he hadn't quite convinced her of that, if she was being truthful. She had never been able to fully believe in the plans for their future on which he'd waxed eloquent now and again.

Liberty gazed out into the swirl of activity outside the window but without really seeing it, lost in her thoughts. She had berated herself often in the months she'd been seeing Gerard for her lack of faith in the permanence of their relationship, telling herself the years of seeing her mother go from man to man had made her cynical, but it hadn't been that.

She frowned slightly as her mind searched for the key to her scepticism and doubt. Gerard was undeniably handsome, sexy, amusing, wealthy and fun to be with, but he had a weak mouth, a mouth that suggested life had been one easy ride for him. It hadn't dawned on her until this moment but now she realised the knowledge had been at the back of her mind for the last few hours, ever since she had gazed into Carter Blake's ruthlessly hard face, in fact. The two men were poles apart.

She twisted on the seat, suddenly immensely irritated with herself. Was she going doolally here? What on earth was she doing, comparing the one with the other anyway? Carter she didn't know from Adam, and Gerard was simply a socialite first and foremost. They both might be socialites for all she knew. Maybe Carter Blake hadn't done a day's work in his life either. Anyway, she certainly didn't want either one of them in her life and why she was wasting one thought on them she didn't know. This night belonged to her father and Joan.

There was even a buzz on the pavement outside the Phoenix; it was that sort of place. A great nightclub with wonderful food, dancing and a floor show—the Phoenix got everything right. Liberty had been to plenty of nightclubs in the past but all too often she found if the band and floor show were good, the food was mediocre, and vice versa.

She had only put one foot onto the pavement when her father appeared like a genie beside her, his face flushed with excitement and his eyes bright. He looked ten years younger. 'Wow!' He took her into his arms, hugging her tight for a moment. 'You look beautiful.'

'You look pretty good yourself,' she said once he had let her breathe again. It was true, he did. The hair which had once been brown was now completely grey but just as thick as ever, and the tall broad-shouldered body was slim and fit. The sum of money her mother had spent to remain looking young and attractive must be into six figures by now, but her father was just getting better and better naturally. Like fine wine.

'Come and meet Joan,' David Fox said after he had paid the taxi driver and taken Liberty's arm in his, leading her through the open front door of the Phoenix with a nod to the two doormen on duty there.

Joan was sitting at the cocktail bar situated just outside the main eating and dancing area, and she left her seat as she caught sight of them. Liberty had almost persuaded herself that her recollection of the woman who had stolen her father's heart must be clouded by a child's vision, but no. Joan was still small, dumpy and ordinary, her rosy cheeks free of make-up and her hairstyle dated. Her father was looking at his old love as though she was Julia Roberts, Catherine Zeta-Jones and Gwyneth Paltrow rolled into one. Suddenly Liberty had a lump in her throat.

'Hello, Liberty,' Joan said quietly.

Joan's wide smile couldn't quite hide the anxiousness in her soft brown eyes, and on the spur of the moment Liberty ignored the other woman's outstretched hand and hugged her instead, her voice warm as she said, 'I'm so pleased to meet you again, Joan, especially now I know what you mean to Dad.'

'You…you don't mind?' It was wary.

'Mind?' Liberty smiled, her gaze including her father as she said, 'You're just what he needs. It's high time he had a little happiness.'

'Thank you, Libby.' Joan had taken her hands and now pressed them, tears glittering in her eyes. 'I can't tell you what it means for you to say that.'

It set the tone for the evening. By the end of the first course of a meal which was truly superb, Liberty found she had totally relaxed and was enjoying herself. She had forgotten—or perhaps, as she'd only been a child when she had first known Joan, she hadn't realised—that Joan had a terrific sense of humour along with a wit that was positively wicked at times. Within a few minutes of being in the other woman's company Liberty could perfectly understand why her father was so captivated by her. And she was the absolute antithesis of Miranda.

It was as Liberty was finishing the last mouthful of her baked scallops with cured back bacon and thyme that her attention was drawn to a table a short distance away. She didn't know quite what had attracted her gaze—maybe it was because the four people about to be seated had caused something of a minor stir, one of the women being a well-known supermodel—but as her mildly enquiring eyes met grey-granite she felt the impact down to her fragile but wildly expensive silver sandals.

Of all the people to see tonight—Carter Blake! As he smiled at her she managed to force a fairly normal smile in return, glad of the three or four tables between them as her heart pounded so hard she was sure he would have noticed if he'd been a little nearer. The contact only lasted a moment or two and Carter was the one to break it, turning to the elegant woman at his side and saying something as they all sat down.

Liberty took a hefty gulp at her wine before she became conscious that her father—in the gregarious way he had with people—was speaking in an undertone to a man at the next table who had also been looking across the room. 'Should we all know who they are?' David Fox asked mildly as the head waiter appeared at Carter's table with a distinctly ingratiating smile.

The other man grinned at him, clearly amused. 'The woman in the red dress is Carmen Lapotiaze,' he said softly, 'the famous—or perhaps it should be infamous—model, and the other woman is an actress, quite well-known.'

'Not by me,' David Fox said cheerfully. 'And the men?'

'The good-looking brute with Carmen is Carter Blake; he owns this place and half of London. The other guy I don't know.'

'He owns this nightclub?' It was Joan who was speaking now and she leant forward interestedly. 'That explains all the scurrying about of the staff then.'

The other man nodded. 'He's one big fish,' he said quietly. 'Rumour has it he has his thumb in umpteen pies; not bad for a man who started with next to nothing a decade or so ago, eh? That's if all the gossip about him can be believed, of course.' He smiled again before turning to the woman with him, a voluptuous brunette who positively dripped diamonds.

'Well, ladies, looks like we chose the right night for a bit of excitement.' David beamed at Joan and his daughter, clearly pleased with himself.

Liberty didn't want to puncture his bubble but she felt she had to say something. 'I'm not so sure about that,' she said with a smile to soften her words. 'The man who ran into me—I'll give you three guesses who it was, but his name begins with B and ends with E.'

'Never!' Her father stared at her. 'You don't mean…'

'And he was driving the most beautiful Mercedes,' Liberty said ruefully. 'Or at least it was until my little car had the temerity to jump out in front of it.'

'Oh, Libby.' Her father had clearly told Joan about the accident because now the other woman put her hand on Liberty's arm. 'Was he okay about it? He isn't going to be awkward, is he? We can leave if you feel uncomfortable.'

'No, not at all,' Liberty said hastily. 'He was very good, actually.' Apart from making her feel two inches tall. Which she had probably thoroughly deserved, she admitted silently, but that didn't make it any easier to take. 'And we couldn't possibly leave without dessert anyway,' she added brightly.

'I do love my puddings.' Joan pulled a face. 'As is pretty obvious. I'd love to be as slim as you but even from a small child I've been this shape.'

'You're a perfect shape,' her father cut in before Liberty could say anything. 'Don't you dare change a thing about yourself, you hear me? I can't abide women who exist on a lettuce leaf all day. My surgery is full of them all saying they've got stress or nerves or whatever, when what they really need is a few suet puddings and a dumpling or two.'

'Oh, David.'

Joan was giggling now, but even as Liberty joined in their laughter she found she was envying the older woman with all her heart. To be loved utterly for yourself by your partner in life—how many women were ever lucky enough to find that? Her work brought her into contact with masses of women who had been dumped for a younger model by their husbands, and it worked the other way too. Her own mother was proof of that. She had made up her mind years ago that true love was a fantasy, something which was warm and comforting and wonderful in novels and fairy tales, but not part of the real world. But now, looking at her father and Joan, she was forced to admit there could be exceptions to the rule. But then her father was special; she'd always known that.

Liberty was very careful not to let her eyes stray to that other table while they continued with their meal, but she found herself draining three glasses of wine for Dutch courage. It was delicious wine—everything was delicious—but as she stood up to go to the ladies cloakroom before their coffee and brandy was served, she realised it was also very potent.

Aware that her vertiginous sandals were more than able to tip her over if she didn't concentrate hard, she made her way to the cloakroom with decorous sedateness, every muscle in her body under rigid control. Wouldn't he just love it if the dopey lamebrain—as she was sure he thought of her—ended up in a pile at his feet, proving she was just as dizzy and empty-headed as he suspected, she told herself bitterly.

Once in the luxurious marble surrounds she gazed about her. She remembered the awe she'd felt on her first visit here and now this was compounded by the knowledge that Carter Blake owned it all. He must be loaded, utterly loaded. Was Carmen Lapotiaze his lover?

She caught at the thought, angry with herself for speculating even as she answered; of course she would be. Probably one of many. Sexual magnetism had literally oozed from the man and there had been a wealth of experience in that rugged face. A tiny shiver curled down her spine and she resolutely banished all further conjecture. Carter Blake was absolutely nothing to do with her and his sex life even less so!

She fiddled with her hair and applied a touch of lipstick before leaving the cloakroom, delaying the moment she had to re-emerge even as she berated her cowardice. She hated to admit it, but every mouthful of food and sip of wine had been accompanied by an almost painful awareness of the tall, dark figure sitting some distance away, and even when she had been conversing with her father and Joan her ears had been tuned in for the laughter which emanated from his table now and again. That was bad enough, but it was all the more galling because he had, no doubt, put her out of his mind immediately after that one brief polite smile. Certainly she didn't think he'd looked her way again.

Her toilette completed, she shut the clasp of her evening bag with a little snap and squared her shoulders. She had already told her father she needed to be at the office early the next morning—which was perfectly true—and that she would be leaving shortly after coffee was finished. The main reason for this was to leave the two lovebirds alone to dance and enjoy themselves, but since Carter had appeared on the scene wild horses wouldn't have kept her in the nightclub.

She opened the door of the cloakroom, stepping out into

the thickly carpeted foyer and then nearly jumping out of her skin as a hand closed over her wrist.

'I'm sorry,' Carter said at the side of her. 'Did I startle you?'

'Of course you startled me,' she said crisply, pulling her arm away and refusing to be intimidated by the height and breadth of him. She also refused to reflect on the fact that, attractive and compelling as he had been earlier that afternoon, he was doubly so in the white tuxedo which sat on the big body with designer ease. 'I'm not used to people creeping up behind me.' She frowned at him to make sure he knew she was serious.

'I don't think I've ever crept in my life,' he answered with a silky amusement which immediately caught her on the raw.

'Really.' She surveyed him through unfriendly brown eyes. 'Look, if you're hoping I've got my details on me, forget it. This bag holds a lipstick and comb and little else.'

He didn't spare the silk purse a glance. Instead he continued to observe her with a scrutiny which was unnerving before he said, 'The accident was your fault, not mine. We've already established that. That being the case, why are you so hostile, Miss Fox?'

Liberty stiffened. 'I don't know what you are talking about. I am most certainly not hostile.'

'No?' The dark face was overtly mocking.

'No.' It was a sharp snap.

She glared at him, and then was further annoyed and taken aback when he laughed softly, his firm mouth curving to reveal even white teeth. 'I blame the hair.'

'What?' He had completely lost her and it showed.

'Red always makes for fireworks,' he drawled easily.

Always? *Always?* He was comparing her to other women he had known, probably even bedded? She drew herself up to her full five feet eight inches, which unfortunately wasn't as commanding as it would have been with a man of lesser height, and said coldly, 'What is it that you want, Mr Blake?'

The black eyebrows rose a fraction. 'What is it you are offering, Miss Fox?'

*Irritating* man! 'You know what I mean,' she said primly.

'I'm not sure I do,' he murmured, studying her angry face with hidden fascination. He had been right about the hair—it *was* glorious. Rich and glowing with a sheen on it like pure silk. And the way it framed her face, bringing out the porcelain quality to that perfect skin and the darkness of her eyes. How could he have thought for a moment she was in any way ordinary?

'You were obviously waiting here for me. Why?'

'You don't think it possible I was passing through to the men's cloakroom and noticed you?' he asked blandly, indicating a door at the far end of the foyer.

She stared at him, suddenly feeling a complete idiot. Again. Something she was getting used to when she was round this man. Why on earth would he be waiting for her when he was with Carmen Lapotiaze? She must have been mad to think it for a second and even crazier to say so. She took a deep breath and prayed her face wasn't as fiery as it felt. Then she didn't know what to say.

Carter decided to put her out of her misery. 'Actually, you were right; I was waiting for you.' He watched her eyes narrow ominously and added hastily, 'I've checked my car and the damage is minimal. If you let me buy you dinner some time we'll forget about insurance companies. And I have a guy who can fix your car for next to nothing, incidentally.'

'I don't understand.' And then the frown of confusion

cleared. Dinner. He'd suggested dinner but it would probably be spelt bed if he was like most of his kind. As her face scorched again, she said icily, 'I think I would prefer to let this go through the right channels, Mr Blake.'

'Why?' he asked in a tone which suggested mild interest.

Well, as he'd asked... 'Because I wouldn't have dinner with you if you were the last man on earth. This might sound like an old cliché, but I'm not that sort of girl. I suggest you get back to your dinner companions, Mr Blake.'

Just a flicker of something she couldn't quite read crossed his face before his features cleared of all expression. 'I said dinner and I meant dinner,' he said softly. 'I've never yet bought a woman, Miss Fox. Surprising as it clearly appears to you, I haven't had to.'

She could believe that. And she knew immediately she had made another huge mistake. Liberty groaned inwardly. 'I'm sorry.' She held his razor-sharp gaze even though she felt like bolting back into the cloakroom. 'I had no right to assume... It's just that most men...' She didn't know how to continue.

'Take advantage of any opportunity to get to know a woman as lovely as you?' A brief smile touched his lips and then disappeared. 'I will plead guilty to that but not the rest. I am not "most men" as you'll find out.'

Over her dead body. She wasn't having anything to do with this man. He was dangerous. In fact, he made poor little Gerard look like a schoolboy in the seduction techniques.

Liberty forced a smile. 'My father's waiting; I have to go,' she said quickly. 'But I will phone and arrange for things to be sorted out.'

'When?' It was immediate, his eyes narrowing.

'What?' The nerve of the man, to try to tie her down like this!

'When will you phone?' he persisted silkily.

She had to get a handle on this, bring it back into the normal sphere of things. She called on all her training to keep cool and objective, or at least to give the appearance of being so. 'Within the next twenty-four hours or so,' she said evenly, refusing to be drawn further. 'Now, as I said, my father is waiting, so if you'll excuse me.'

'There's no rush; it isn't as if he is sitting there alone. Is that your mother with him?' For the first time since his teens Carter found himself trying to make conversation with a woman who clearly wanted shot of him. It astounded him. He half-expected her to tell him to mind his own business or to go to hell, but she did neither, merely staring at him with big brown eyes. Brown eyes as soft and velvety as a doe at bay.

'No,' she said finally. 'She is not my mother.'

His lips twitched. Polite but firm, even though every line and curve of her body suggested she would rather be anywhere else than here. He ignored the screaming body language, saying quietly, 'I didn't think so. I couldn't see any resemblance between you.'

Liberty shrugged. 'There's none between my mother and I, as it happens. She's a small, blue-eyed blonde.'

Now it was Carter who stared. He had sensed something when she had spoken of her mother—very definite vibes and none of them good. Maybe it would be better if she didn't ring him, after all; the last thing he needed right now was to get mixed up with a woman who came with baggage. He liked his relationships with women to emulate the way he viewed acquiring and disposing of a car—they needed to be good together while it lasted but once the parting of the ways came it was all straightforward. So it was with some surprise he heard himself say, 'I'll escort you back to your table.'

'No need.' Liberty was determined the last thing she was going to do was introduce him to her father and Joan. 'Your dinner companion might get the wrong idea.'

'Carmen? Oh no, Carmen and I understand each other very well,' he said nonchalantly.

Funny, but she didn't doubt that for a minute!

Liberty wasn't aware her face was revealing her thoughts until the big body bent closer. 'Carmen and I are just good friends, Liberty,' he said pleasantly, but with a touch of steel in his voice which indicated he hadn't appreciated her supposition. 'If there was anything else between us I wouldn't have suggested taking you to dinner. I've never pretended to be a hearth and home guy, but one woman at a time is more than enough for me. Okay?' Dark eyebrows rose mockingly.

She felt furious that he had somehow put her in the wrong. He had walked in with that woman draped all over him like poison ivy and now he was blaming her for putting two and two together and making five. She tilted her head back and looked him straight in the eye. 'Your association with Miss Lapotiaze, or anyone else for that matter, is absolutely nothing to do with me,' she said clearly. 'Goodnight, Mr Blake.' And she left him before he had a chance to react, walking as swiftly as her inordinately high heels would allow into the heart of the nightclub.

She had half-expected him to follow her or to try to catch hold of her again, but she reached the others without incident—apart from almost going headlong across the table as her heel caught in the hem of her dress at the last moment.

Her father and Joan smiled at her with the guilty look of two people who had just been whispering sweet nothings, and she smiled brightly back, wondering how soon she could make her excuses and leave. Why had she allowed Carter to get under her skin like that? she asked herself as she sipped at her coffee. No other man had ever affected her in such a way. Not that there had been many men in her past.

The coffee was burning her throat but she barely felt it, her whole body tuned as tight as piano wire. She had had plenty of dates before Gerard, of course, but she had always kept things casual, and even Gerard hadn't actually broken her heart. Bruised it maybe, and crushed her pride into the ground, but she couldn't in all honesty say she was devastated beyond measure by his betrayal.

Her eyes opened wide as the knowledge dawned that she was well and truly over him and it had only taken a matter of weeks. Was that awful? She considered the matter and then decided she didn't care if it was. She was just so thankful she hadn't gone the whole hog and slept with him as he had been nagging at her to do for the last couple of months of their relationship. She would have hated to be another notch on his worn-away bedpost. When, or maybe that should be if, she gave herself to a man she at least wanted it to mean something for both of them.

When she made her move to leave, her father insisted on coming with her to the entrance of the nightclub and standing with her while the doorman hailed her a cab. 'Thanks for being so nice to Joan.' He hugged her as he spoke, his voice thick. 'Do you think it would be rushing it if I asked her to marry me soon? And I mean real soon,' he added somewhat bashfully.

'After twenty odd years?' Liberty reached up and patted his face, her touch gentle. 'Go for it, Dad, if you're sure.'

'I've never been surer of anything in my life.'

'Then ask her. Life's too short to dilly-dally.'

'You'd come to the ceremony? It'll only be a register office do, I suppose, but I'd like you there,' he said urgently.

'You try and keep me away,' said Liberty as the black cab pulled up in front of them. 'Now, go back to her and I'll give you a ring in the morning. And thanks for a lovely evening.'

He stood and waved her off as he had done on countless occasions in the past, but this time they both knew it was different. The cab got held up at the traffic lights, and as Liberty turned and looked through the back window she saw him bound back into the club like a twenty-year-old.

She smiled to herself, glad for him and for Joan too, but somehow their delight in each other had made her restless. Or was it something else, some*one* else, who had caused her to feel all at odds with the world tonight? She frowned, loath to admit Carter Blake could have such an influence on her when she had only met him a few hours ago.

It wasn't him, she had decided firmly by the time the cab had deposited her home. It was the whole day—seeing her mother, the accident, the awful afternoon at work and then encountering Carter again on an evening when her emotions had been running high anyway. A good night's sleep and everything would be back in perspective again. Anything else was just not an option.

## CHAPTER THREE

LIBERTY rang Carter Blake at nine o'clock the next evening. She figured that was late enough to suggest she hadn't been champing at the bit, even though the wretched man had been at the forefront of her mind all day. She couldn't remember an occasion when she had had to check and recheck her work—she was normally utterly focused and concentrated—but the day had been a nightmare of errors and slip-ups, and all because of one grey-eyed man who wouldn't stay in the box she had designated for him in her mind. And she hated that. She really *hated* it.

She rang the land-line number he had given her rather than the mobile, praying that an answering machine would cut in enabling her to parrot off her details without speaking to him. At least that was what she told herself she was praying for, refusing to acknowledge the curling excitement in the pit of her stomach at the thought of hearing that rich, deep voice again.

It was with something of an anticlimax, therefore, when the phone was picked up at the other end and a female voice said, 'Jennifer Blake. Can I help you?'

His mother? But the voice sounded too young. His *wife*? No, he hadn't had the look of a man who was married. And then she told herself not to be so ridiculous. Women the whole world over were fooled by men who didn't look or behave as though they were married! As her work proved daily.

Liberty cleared her throat carefully. 'This is Liberty Fox. I'm ringing to—'

'Oh, yes, Carter told me you might ring. Hang on a mo, I'll just call him.'

'No, that's not necessary. If you'll—' But she was talking to thin air. She could hear someone calling Carter in the background and her heart increased its rapid beat until she felt as though it was banging against her ribcage.

There was a few seconds pause, and then she heard a click which meant an extension had been picked up. 'Liberty?' The deep voice sent goose pimples all over her body. 'I've been waiting for your call.'

She wrinkled her brow. What did that mean? Was it just a polite way of starting the conversation or did he mean he really *had* been waiting to hear from her again? It was safer to assume the former. She took a deep breath. 'I've got those details you wanted, Mr Blake,' she said formally.

'Carter.' It was pleasant but firm.

'I beg your pardon?' She hoped she didn't sound fluttery.

'You've caused some scratches on my immaculate paintwork,' he drawled easily. 'The least you can do is to come down off your high horse and call me by name.'

She opened her mouth to reply but then he added, 'And you can put the phone down in the hall now, Jen.' There was no answer to this but the phone was replaced with a definite click. 'My sister,' he said mockingly. 'My very nosy sister.'

'Oh, right.' For some reason she wasn't sure of why she hadn't thought of siblings. He seemed such a one-off somehow.

'Now, perhaps you can start off by giving me your telephone number and address?' The smoky voice was suddenly brisk and matter-of-fact and it took her by surprise.

'Yes, of course.' She rattled off the information, but when she got to the insurance details he stopped her.

'I don't need your registration number or insurance company, Liberty,' he said quietly. 'Not for a dinner date.'

Her heart gave up trying to escape through her chest and jumped up into her throat. 'I… I don't think…' Her voice sounded as though she was choking. She coughed, telling herself to get a grip. 'I thought we had agreed that wasn't an option,' she said firmly.

'No. You made a very unkind supposition as to my motives for asking you out which I think I corrected in such a way as to clear the air,' he returned pleasantly. 'That being the case, I can see no reason why we can't have an enjoyable evening in each other's company.'

It sounded so reasonable. She frowned. So there had to be a catch somewhere. 'I'm afraid I'm working hard at the moment,' she said carefully, 'so I'm not dating.'

'With the normal, run of the mill man, maybe. But I'm different.' It was supremely arrogant, and even when he qualified the outrageous statement with, 'I'm different because you owe me, Liberty. You did cause the accident, remember? I might have been badly hurt,' imperiousness was still paramount.

'You weren't.' She suspected a ten ton truck would make no impact on Carter Blake, let alone her little car.

'I said I might have been. Think what a shock it was to have a car suddenly leap out in front of me like that. A lesser man might have had a heart attack on the spot.'

Involuntarily she smiled, and then was thankful he couldn't see his charm was working. No doubt he always had women falling down like ninepins with one lift of his eyebrows! She schooled her voice to hide any amusement as she said, 'You didn't have a heart attack and the only thing that was hurt was my car—with a few scratches on yours which I've already said I'll pay for,' she added quickly.

'I don't want you to pay. I want you to have dinner with me.'

She put a hand to her brow. If she related this conversation to anyone else they would think she was stark staring mad not to snap his hand off. Repairs to a Mercedes' paintwork wouldn't be cheap, she hadn't fooled herself about that, but... She swallowed hard. He clearly wasn't going to take no for an answer; that was the bottom line. She might just as well agree to see him once and then that would be that. 'All right, I'll have dinner with you,' she said a touch ungraciously.

He didn't comment on her churlishness. 'Good.' There was a wealth of satisfaction in his voice. 'Tomorrow being Saturday you'll have all day to get ready.'

'Hang on, I didn't say I was free tomorrow,' she protested immediately. How dared he assume she was at his beck and call?

'Are you?' he enquired pleasantly.

'Yes, as it happens, but I might not have been,' she said, knowing she sounded unnecessarily belligerent.

'You said you weren't dating at the moment.' His voice was insultingly patient, as though he was talking to a recalcitrant child. 'That being the case, I assumed the most important thing you might have on was washing your hair.'

'I also said I was working hard,' she pointed out tartly. 'I might have had a schedule I couldn't change.'

'You'd still have to eat some time,' he said reasonably.

She gave up. She had the feeling that Carter Blake always won an argument and maybe it was better to get it over and done with.

He'd assumed victory because he carried on with barely a pause. 'I'll pick you up at seven, okay? And you needn't dress up too much. The restaurant I'm taking you to is smart casual with the emphasis on excellent food.'

'Right.' She'd assumed they would be dining at the Phoenix but he'd obviously got something else in mind. She hesitated a moment before saying, 'Thank you.' It was grudging.

'My pleasure,' Carter replied, his voice holding only the faintest trace of amusement. 'Goodnight, Liberty.'

'Goodnight.' She put down the telephone in something of a daze and sat staring at it for a full minute before she could persuade herself to move. And not for the world would she have admitted to herself that she'd known all along that Carter would get his way and that, moreover, she had wanted him to.

Her mind had still been buzzing when she went to bed, but contrary to what she'd expected Liberty awoke the next morning after a deep, satisfying sleep. She lay for some minutes in the warmth of her double bed, gazing across the room at the picture she had bought when she'd first moved into the house. She had seen it in a little art gallery round the corner from the office and had fallen in love with it immediately, knowing she had to have it even though it had been wildly expensive at a time when she was watching every penny.

The snowy garden depicted was beautifully painted, the setting sun turning the snow rosy pink in parts, but it was the two figures to the forefront of the picture which always brought an aching warmth into her chest. The mother was kneeling in the snow with her arms wide open to receive the laughing little girl running to meet her, the snowman the child had been working on watching with a benevolent smile on his white face.

She didn't know why she loved it so much because it always made her want to cry, but maybe it was the love shining out of the woman's face that gripped her heart each time she looked at the picture. Whatever, she'd known she had to have it, and when she had shown it to her father the first night she had cooked him dinner in her new home and he'd said, 'Laying a few ghosts, eh, sweetheart?' it had bothered her for days.

She would never have children. She continued to stare at the picture as her eyes clouded. Much as she longed to be a mother one day, she would never trust herself or any children to one man. Marriage, commitment, faithfulness, they just didn't work in the real world, and all children should have two parents who were devoted to them and who loved each other too. A couple of her friends who were disillusioned with men had made the decision to become single mothers, but that wasn't for her either. She had been brought up by a single parent—her father—and she knew he would be the first to say it was not ideal.

But she would make a good life for herself—she *was* making a good life for herself. She twisted in the bed, suddenly irritated with the way her thoughts had gone. She had her home and a great job, and she intended to develop her career and take it as far as she could. In a few years junior partner, and eventually rising right up the ladder. The declaration didn't hold the same thrill it usually did.

'Coffee.' She spoke out loud, flinging back the covers and leaping out of bed. 'Coffee and toast and a long read of the paper.' A leisurely start to the day was her weekend treat to herself after the mad scramble of Monday to Friday.

She was on her second cup of coffee, curled up on one of the sofas in the sitting room, when the telephone rang at her elbow. She lifted the receiver automatically, still reading.

'Liberty?' The deep, rich voice brought her jerking upwards with dire consequences. It was fortunate the coffee had had a chance to cool down a little because most of it ended up in her lap. 'It's Carter.'

He'd reconsidered. He was going to cancel their date and she really couldn't blame him, she thought feverishly, mopping at her silk pyjamas with a handkerchief she'd had in her pocket. It was a moment or two before she managed a breathless, 'Yes?'

There followed a longish pause. 'Are you alone?' he asked abruptly, his voice a shade cooler.

'What?' She stared at the phone in surprise.

'I said, are you alone?' he repeated impatiently.

'It's nine o'clock in the morning,' she said bewilderedly. 'Of course I'm alone.'

'You sound…different.'

So would you if you'd had half a cup of coffee in a sensitive place. She took a deep breath. 'I've only just woken up,' she said, stretching a point. There was no way she was going to tell him about the coffee. And then, as the implication behind his words dawned, she snapped, 'And what do you mean by asking me if I'm alone anyway? Who on earth did you think was here?'

She could almost picture him shrug as he said mildly, 'I've no idea, Liberty. You're a single woman; you're entitled to have anyone in your home.'

'Look, Carter, let's get one thing straight,' she said sharply. 'I'm not into one-night stands or anything else of that nature if it comes to that. I sleep alone, okay? Always.'

'Always?'

'Always.' She could almost see the disbelief on his face.

'Right.' The briefest of pauses and then, 'I'm glad to hear it,' he said flatly.

He didn't actually sound very pleased. Suddenly she felt better. Put a spoke into his plans for this evening, had she?

What a shame. Was he getting a glimmer that the big seduction scene wouldn't cut any ice with her? 'So? Why are you calling?' she asked forthrightly. 'Remembered you're busy elsewhere tonight? Urgent business of some kind, is it?'

'Don't be silly,' he said without finesse.

Liberty blinked. Charming.

'And don't be so defensive,' he added more softly.

'I'm not defensive,' she said defensively before biting her lip hard. Irritating man. Always had to be right.

'I'm ringing to see if you're free this afternoon as well as this evening, actually,' he went on. 'And, before you come up with a whole lot of excuses, I've suddenly acquired two tickets for a matinée in the West End.'

He mentioned a show she had been dying to see for ages but which was booked solid for months, and Liberty stared at the phone as though it was at fault. It *would* have to be something she just couldn't refuse, wouldn't it. 'That sounds nice,' she said carefully. 'If you're sure you don't want to take someone else.'

'Don't get too excited.' It was mordant. 'I'll pick you up at one o'clock.'

He didn't even give her a chance to say goodbye before he put the phone down.

She changed three times before one o'clock, but when the doorbell sounded and she gave a final glance in the mirror she was satisfied the alpaca tweed coat worn over a cashmere ivory polo-neck minidress would do for both the theatre and the restaurant later. And the dress had always particularly suited her.

She was wearing the minimum of make-up, just a dusting of ivory eyeshadow to highlight her eyes and a little mascara, and she had decided to pull her hair back into a knot on top of her head. It was a somewhat severe hairstyle for the weekend but somehow she felt it sent a message after their earlier conversation, a re-emphasis that she was not up for grabs. She wrinkled her nose at herself. If he could have women like Carmen on his arm she really didn't know why he was bothering with her in the first place. Perhaps his intentions were strictly honourable and above board, but just in case…

'Hi.' He presented her with a bunch of flowers as she opened the door, bending closer to her, and she smelled the faint scent of sharp lemony aftershave. It was a very male smell and frighteningly seductive. The big body was clothed in charcoal trousers and a black leather jacket and was even more seductive. She tried very hard not to think about that.

'Hello.' She took the flowers and then realised they meant she had to ask him in. 'Take a seat for a moment while I put these in water, and—' belatedly she remembered her manners '—thank you,' she added a little stiffly.

He looked all shoulders and muscle and endless legs, and he grinned at her. She had noticed before how his smile mellowed the hard planes and valleys of his strong face, and his voice was smokier than ever when he said, 'My pleasure,' before glancing around. 'This is nice,' he said appreciatively. 'Have you lived here long?'

'Not really.' Ridiculous, but she found she didn't want to share any details of her life. He had already made inroads into her safe little world as it was. 'Do take a seat.'

She hurried down to the kitchen, grabbing the first vase that came to hand and stuffing the fragrant bunch of freesias, cream roses and baby's breath into it with scant regard for display. She fairly leapt up the stairs to the sitting room, plonking the vase down on the coffee table in the middle of the room as she said, 'They're lovely but you shouldn't have. Shall we go? We don't want to be late.'

He looked a little startled at her eagerness but strolled across to the door, opening it for her and then standing aside as she passed him. Her shoulder brushed against him as she exited the house, and she felt the brief contact down to her toes. She had hoped he hadn't noticed the little start she gave, but as he joined her on the top of the steps and watched as she shut the front door, he said, 'Relax, Liberty, for crying out loud. You're like a cat on a hot tin roof. You're not still worrying I'm going to demand payment for those scratches to my Merc in the age-old way, are you?'

She flushed hotly, turning to face him after locking the door and slipping the keys into her handbag. 'Of course not,' she said with what she hoped was scathing contempt.

'Good,' he said, his stone-grey eyes running over her pink face. Where had she been all her life that she could blush at such a relatively innocuous remark? He knew a great many women who wouldn't blush at the most explicit bawdiness. Where did she hide herself away during the day? A library, perhaps? Yes, he could see her as a demure librarian when she had her hair this way. Or working with young children in a nursery maybe. Or even a dusty little bookshop somewhere? 'What do you do?' he asked abruptly as they descended the steps together. 'For your job, I mean.'

'I'm a solicitor,' she said expressionlessly. 'I specialise in civil litigation and crime at the moment.'

He stopped dead on the pavement.

'What?' She stared up at him. 'What's the matter?'

'You're a woman full of surprises, Liberty Fox,' he said softly, reaching out and loosening the slides holding her hair as he spoke. 'As I'm beginning to find out.'

'Don't.' As she felt her hair fall down about her shoulders she tried to retrieve the slides, but he merely pocketed them, a strange look on his face.

'I'd like those back please,' she said firmly.

'Don't hide your light under a bushel,' he said shortly.

She cleared her suddenly dry throat. Something in his eyes made her short of breath. She decided to forget about the slides.

A cab was waiting at the kerb and after Carter had given the name of the theatre he opened the door and helped her in, sitting down beside her a moment later. His long legs were stretched out in front of him and he looked supremely relaxed. She bitterly resented his composure considering she felt a bundle of nerves.

'Now.' He took her arm and tucked it in his as though they had known each other for months. 'Tell me a bit about yourself,' he said easily, his voice warm.

She was too shocked at first to remove her arm and then, when the butterflies had settled a little, it seemed too late so she left it where it was. 'There's nothing much to tell,' she prevaricated warily. 'Just the usual boring stuff.'

'Somehow I doubt that.' The eyebrows quirked a little.

Well, it was the truth. Did he think she had a torrid past or some major catastrophe she had fought to triumph over? She glanced at him, her eyes focusing on his mouth, which was firm and faintly stern. It was a strong mouth, hard. It would kiss wonderfully... She went a little hot, whether because of her thoughts or the feel of his thigh next to hers she wasn't sure. 'I assure you I'm very run of the mill,' she said carefully. 'Thirty years old, love my job, love my home—'

'Ever been married?' he asked casually.

'Married?' She stared at him in amazement. 'Of course not.' How old did she look, for goodness' sake?

'There's no of course about it,' he said easily. 'I know loads of women who have been married and divorced by your age, my sister for one.'

Liberty didn't quite know what to say to that, but as she was becoming more acquainted with his body with every tiny bump and jerk the cab gave it was the least of her worries.

Carter smiled faintly to himself. He had sensed the tenseness she was trying to hide along with the reason for it, and found it reassuring that she was at least aware of him as a man. For a time he had wondered if she was unaffected by him, but now he did not think so. For himself, he was surprised just how much he wanted her. It had been years since he'd ached with a combination of lust and uncertainty—since his first girlfriend, in fact, when he had been a callow seventeen years of age—but something about this russet-haired woman had had him tossing and turning all night.

'So,' he said lazily, shifting in the seat slightly just to feel her softness, 'not married then. Ever come close?'

She wished this cab ride would end. She felt as though she was beginning to melt. 'I thought so, not so long ago actually, but it would have been a huge mistake.'

'Oh, yes?' His voice didn't betray the interest which had gripped him. 'The guy in question didn't measure up?'

'He wasn't what he portrayed himself to be,' she said briefly, adding, when he said nothing, 'certainly not in the fidelity stakes anyway and that's something that's set in concrete with me.'

He nodded but did not pursue the subject, for which she was grateful, beginning instead to chat about the forthcoming show and how he had acquired the tickets from a friend who had had to go abroad on business unexpectedly.

Gradually Liberty relaxed a little. She even found

herself smiling once or twice as he set out to amuse her, and by the time they arrived at the theatre she was in the process of reviewing her opinion of him. True, he was too arrogant for comfort, and whatever he said she suspected his ultimate purpose was more than a goodnight kiss, but she could handle those things.

As he helped her out of the cab with the old-fashioned courtesy which was so unexpectedly attractive, she smiled her thanks, watching him as he paid the driver. He was funny and witty and charming, and—much as she hated to admit it—it was delicious to be with a man who was so unapologetically male.

Gerard had been good-looking but in a boyish way, and he hadn't had Carter's—she searched her mind for the right word to describe his appeal—authority, a certain something which was extra to his sex appeal and just as powerfully compelling.

Their seats at the theatre were excellent and the show was great, although in the interval when Liberty found herself pressed a mite too close to Carter in the crush at the bar, she couldn't help but colour up. He didn't appear to notice her agitation, chatting unconcernedly with a coolness she could only envy as her breathing floundered every so often.

The restaurant was only a couple of streets away from the theatre, and when they emerged into a crisp October evening which even the city fumes couldn't spoil and Carter suggested they walk, Liberty jumped at the idea after sitting down all afternoon.

'Hungry?' As he took her hand in his the action was easy and natural and self-assured, and didn't necessitate the bolt of lightning which shot up her arm.

Liberty frowned to herself as they strolled along amid late-night shoppers. What was the matter with her, for goodness' sake? She was a grown woman, not a nervous little schoolgirl out on her first date. The thing was, she didn't want him to think... The frown deepened. What didn't she want him to think? That he was on to a good thing?

She caught sight of her reflection in a shop window and hastily straightened her face before Carter saw her knitted brow. He thought she was crazy enough already.

But he hadn't made a pass at her, she reasoned silently, or given her any reason to think he was going to come on strong in a way which would be offensive. She'd had the odd date in the past who had tried it on and she had more than coped anyway. But then she had always known she was in control with those guys, able to put them in their place with the biting sarcasm she could produce as a defence when necessary. Carter wasn't like that. Perhaps that was why she was so jittery?

Or perhaps it was because she was longing for him to kiss her, to see how it would be? The little voice at the back of her mind shocked her but she couldn't deny it. He fascinated her. She didn't want him to, but he was just so, so... She gave up trying to find a word to describe him because they were approaching the restaurant.

'Here we are.' He paused just before the entrance, smiling down at her with unfathomable eyes. 'I hope you enjoy it here. The owner's a friend of mine, and the old adage "to be an especially good cook you have to sprinkle love and passion into your food" certainly applies in Adam's case. He doesn't go in for pomp or ceremony but everything he makes tastes terrific.'

She was staring up at him as she listened, and when he suddenly bent, skimming her mouth with his lips, it was all over before she had a chance to react. He had opened the door of the restaurant in the next moment anyway, and

all she could do was to step forward when he stood aside
for her to enter.

His mouth had been firm and warm and the brief contact
had been pleasant, very pleasant. As a tall, dark man came
hurrying towards them, all Liberty could think about was
what it would be like if they had been somewhere quiet
and secluded and he had really meant business. She pulled
herself together fast and forced her errant thoughts into
order as the man in front of her grinned at Carter. 'Carter,
you old reprobate,' he said jovially, reaching out and taking one of Carter's hands in both of his. 'You always know
when griddled lamb chump is on the menu.' And then the
dark eyes turned to Liberty. 'I don't think I've had the
pleasure…' he added smoothly, bowing slightly.

'Cut the charm, Adam,' Carter said amusedly. 'It
doesn't work with Liberty. I should know; I've tried hard
enough.' He turned smiling eyes on her. 'Liberty Fox meet
Adam Temple—scoundrel, miscreant and all round
Lothario, but a chef second to none.'

Adam didn't seem the least put out by the introduction.
'Liberty will make up her own mind about me, won't you,
Liberty?' he said softly, bending from the waist and kissing her hand in a Latin gesture which went with the coal-
black hair and dark eyes which danced wickedly as they
met her amused ones.

'I always do.' She smiled at both men, glad the little
scene had given her time to get her fluttering nerves under
control.

'I'm glad to hear it.' Adam straightened, nodding his
head towards Carter. 'Fathomed him yet?'

'She hasn't had time,' Carter cut in evenly. 'We only
met two days ago. Now, about that table, Adam.'

Adam took the hint and smilingly showed them to the
back of the restaurant where a small alcove seated a cosy

table for two in a position where one could see but not be seen. There was a small candle alight in the middle of the table and the crisp white cloth and napkins were of fine linen, but the overall ambience of the place was very different from the plush luxury of the Phoenix.

Adam having disappeared back into the kitchens, the waiter appeared with the wine list and menu, along with a tray holding two cocktails. 'With the compliments of Mr Temple, sir,' he said to Carter, placing the drinks in front of them with some ceremony. 'I'll leave you for a few moments to read and digest and then I'll come back for your order.'

When they were alone again, Carter lifted his glass in a toast. 'To getting to know each other better,' he said, and he did not smile, his eyes tight on her face.

Liberty stared at him. She didn't want to get to know Carter better, and yet on the other hand there was nothing she wanted more. Which made her…crazy. Yes, definitely crazy. She raised her own glass. 'To this evening.' It was sufficiently bland to pass for agreement to his toast, and yet at the same time a statement of limited intent.

She saw the hard mouth twitch but decided to ignore his amusement. 'This is delicious,' she added as she tasted the drink. 'What is it?'

'A Vodkatini. No one does them quite like Adam's man. Most places try to rush the process and that's fatal.'

When Liberty lifted enquiring eyebrows, he continued, 'First one fills a mixing glass with ice and then stirs with a spoon until the glass is chilled. Then tip the ice away, top up with more ice and add a dash or two of dry vermouth whilst still stirring. With me so far?'

His voice was smoky and she blinked. The little table was intimate, how intimate she hadn't realised till now when he bent forward, his eyes stroking her flushed face.

'After that one strains the liquid away and tops up with more ice. Add a large measure of vodka and stir continuously until the vodka is thoroughly chilled. Very importantly, don't chip the ice or the vodka will become diluted. One needs an experienced but tender touch, a subtle caressing of the contents.'

She blinked again. How could he make it sound so sexy?

'Then strain into a frosted martini glass and garnish with lemon zest, and hey presto, a delicious, slightly decadent and innocently lethal drink.' He smiled slowly.

He relaxed back fully into his seat and she felt as though she had been released from something which had held her mind and body in a sensuous warmth.

'I've seen folk downing Vodkatinis like lemonade and then suffering the consequences,' he added conversationally.

Folk? Did that translate into women? His women? Did he bring many other women here? Liberty didn't like the way her mind was firing questions and picked up her menu, opening it and running her eyes over the contents. 'There's a wonderful choice,' she said evenly, determined to bring things to order.

'I can particularly recommend the almond and saffron soup with pimenton roast tomatoes and, of course, the griddle lamb chump with butter beans and apple allioli,' Carter said lazily, draining his glass before he said, 'If we go for that there's a nice Californian merlot that's rich and dark and spicy. If you like red wine, that is.'

'Your favourites, I take it?' she asked coolly.

'Just so.'

'They sound fine by me.' She put down her menu.

Dark eyebrows rose just the slightest. 'Careful,' he said

mildly. 'You'll fool me into thinking you're a nice sub-
missive female after all.'

Liberty sent him a quick but lethal glance just as the
waiter approached.

When the food came it was truly superb. The soup was
the kind of stuff dreams were made of, and the lamb
melted in the mouth. The creamy coffee and praline gateau
Liberty chose for dessert was so light it fairly floated into
her mouth, layers of mascarpone and coffee filling topped
with shards of crunchy praline giving the cake a taste that
was heavenly.

In spite of her enjoyment of the excellent dishes,
however, Liberty knew her taste buds weren't giving full
homage to the food. She was too jittery, too wound up.
Admittedly, Carter was an interesting and amusing companion, the easy charm and wit beguiling, but that was just
it. She'd had her fill of men who were sophisticated and
smooth and slick. Gerard had mastered all those attributes
and look where that had got her. But whereas Gerard had
really been a tinsel and glitter socialite, she sensed there
was much, much more to Carter. There was a vital, almost
dangerous energy about him which both repelled and
attracted her, the more so when it was under rein like now.
But was she playing with fire here? What was the inner
man really like?

As she swallowed the last morsel of the gateau she shivered suddenly, although she couldn't have said why.
Nerves, she supposed.

Adam came over again as they were savouring coffee
and brandies, pulling up a chair and sitting with them for
a short while. He and Carter engaged in an amusing, sharp
and quick-fire banter which emphasised the fact they had
known each other for a long time, and which had Liberty

laughing helplessly more than once. She found she liked the other man very much.

When the restaurant owner left them again, kissing her hand in farewell as he made an extravagant compliment about her appearance, Liberty said quietly, 'How long have you known him? You're clearly very good friends.'

'Adam? We grew up together, he and his sister and myself and Jen. It was a pretty rough housing estate on the outskirts of London, the sort of place where kids either go into crime and drugs or fight to make it in a big way. No happy mediums.'

'And you made it.'

'That we did.' Carter nodded slowly but there was no arrogance in the gesture. 'Three of us at least. Barbara, Adam's sister, died last year of a drug overdose. We all thought she had been clean for years and maybe she was, but sometimes the pull is too great. She and Adam didn't have the big advantage Jen and I had, that's the thing.'

'Which was?' she asked curiously, fascinated by the story.

'Good parents and a secure family life.'

Liberty's eyes widened. He was full of surprises. 'Are they still living there—your parents, I mean?'

He shook his head. 'Once I could afford it I took them out of it. They're in a bungalow by the coast now; they both love the sea and they've always got some friends or other visiting.'

The warmth in his voice as he spoke about his parents touched her far more than she would have liked. 'But your sister lives with you?' she said quietly.

'Temporarily. It was a tough divorce and she took it hard. She's having a breathing space before she looks for a place of her own.' He paused, his voice hardening as he said, 'Everyone could see he was less than the dust under her feet except Jen. The guy was looking for an easy meal ticket and thought by marrying into the Blake name he'd made it. The crunch came when she found out he was messing around with other women. He lived to regret it.'

Liberty stared into the uncompromisingly tough face. She could be wrong but she had the idea that he meant more by that last remark than the fact that his brother-in-law—ex-brother-in-law—had lost his wife. 'Your sister doesn't see him any more then?'

He smiled a smile that had all the warmth of a frozen lake. 'No, she doesn't see him any more,' he said softly. 'The guy values his kneecaps so he keeps away. No doubt he'll latch on to some other gullible female when the dust settles.'

Liberty thought it prudent not to voice the thought that this man must have had a certain amount of guts—or be stark staring crazy—to think he could mess with Carter Blake's sister in the first place. She nodded; it was easier than having to think of a suitable comment.

'And you?' He smiled a real smile this time that made her stomach roll over. 'We've established you're footloose and fancy-free, and I gathered from the other night your parents are not together.'

She really couldn't refuse to discuss her family when she had questioned him about his. She wasn't aware she had stiffened a little but Carter, watching her with intent eyes, was. And he waited with interest to hear what she had to say.

'No, they're not.' It was too succinct and she forced herself to go on. 'They divorced when I was quite young. My…my mother went off with someone else and left my father and I. That was several husbands ago now,' she added, trying for a lightness which didn't quite come off.

Carter expelled a quiet breath. He knew of women—his

own secretary for one—who would have given everything they possessed for a child of their own and yet they'd been told it was not possible, whereas others who couldn't care a fig had them as easily as falling off a log. Nature played the cruellest of all her tricks in this area.

Her tight face and wary eyes warned him not to continue, but his curiosity about this pale-skinned, russet-haired woman was too strong. 'Tough start,' he said evenly, allowing only a smidgen of sympathy to show in his voice. 'Did you get on with your father?'

'He's a wonderful man and I didn't miss out on a thing,' she said proudly, her chin rising. 'Not a thing.'

That wasn't what he had asked. His eyes narrowed. 'Any brothers or sisters?' he asked expressionlessly.

She shook her head, causing the veil of reddish-brown to shimmer and move in the light of the candle. His lower stomach tightened and he felt himself harden.

'My mother isn't a maternal woman,' she said carefully, stating the obvious, 'and my father's a GP and was always too busy with his job and caring for me to meet someone else. Until now,' she added after a brief pause. 'Now he has someone.'

'The lady in the restaurant?'

She nodded but didn't expand further.

'So how has all that made you feel about love, marriage, family life?' he asked coolly. 'Envious or cynical?'

She couldn't believe he'd asked her such a personal question when she hadn't known him for two minutes, and yet she wasn't altogether surprised either. Straight for the jugular. That would be Carter Blake all over, at work and at play.

She finished the last of her now cold coffee before she replied, replacing the cup in the saucer with deliberate coolness before she looked into the male face. 'It's fine for people who want it,' she said grimly. 'Who think they need it.'

'Meaning you don't?' he asked very softly.

She was struggling here but she was blowed if she'd let him see. She shrugged slender shoulders, very aware of the granite eyes fixed on her face as she said, 'Meaning I don't think it is a viable proposition for two people to remain faithful to each other for life and, unless it is, I don't think it's fair to bring children into the relationship.'

For thirty-six years Carter had believed himself to be an autonomous being who worked and played better when there was no question of emotional attachment. He had never really questioned whether he believed in marriage; his parents had been happily wrapped up in each other for nearly forty years despite illness, poverty and everything else life had flung against them in the early days, so he guessed he believed in the concept at least, but he'd always known it was not for him.

From his earliest memory he had been determined to get out of the grime and muck and make something of himself, to rise high, and he'd accepted that to do that he had to be utterly focused. When he'd made his first million he had decided he actually liked the lack of emotional clutter in his life, and that from being a necessity to achieve his goals it was now a free choice.

To be able to take off at a minute's notice, to be answerable to no one with no ties and commitments—he enjoyed that. He *really* enjoyed it. So why, that being the case, should he now have the desire to argue against every principle he'd lived his life by to date? he asked himself irritably. Nevertheless, he found himself saying, 'So you've come down on the side of cynicism rather than envy. Right?'

She didn't argue with him. 'Probably,' she agreed shortly. 'But you asked me how I felt.'

She was right, he had. 'You're saying you would voluntarily choose a solitary lifestyle?' Well you have, the voice outside himself pointed out sharply, and when he answered it with, But I'm a man, that's different, he felt instantly appalled at himself. Both in his work life and his love life he had always held to the view that women were equal with men in every way, and it was galling to discover he was as male chauvinist at heart as the next man. More than galling.

Liberty brushed back her hair with a steady hand, annoyed at the covert criticism she'd caught in his tone but determined to remain outwardly unmoved. 'I'm saying unless two people are absolutely sure their relationship is for life, children shouldn't be brought into it, that's all,' she reiterated firmly. 'My personal opinion, okay? Everyone is entitled to one.'

He had been right back there at the Phoenix; her mother had damaged her all right. 'My parents have been happily married for forty years.' Even as he said it, he wondered why he had.

She obviously wondered the same thing. There was a slight pause and then she said, 'Good. That's very nice for them.'

He settled back in his seat, the harsh angles of his face mellowing as he grinned at her. 'Actually, I agree with you,' he said mildly. 'They probably make up about two per cent of the population and the rest are as miserable as hell.'

'I didn't say that,' she protested.

'But you thought it.' The eyebrows rose mockingly.

Yes, she had, along with the fact that he seemed the sort of man who would be married to his business all his life with no time or patience for a wife and children. Lovers, now that was different. She was sure he would always find time to indulge his physical needs and, like everything else in his life, he would make sure he did it expertly and with finesse. She suddenly felt uncomfortably warm and her voice was slightly breathless when she said, 'We've found something we agree about then?'

'So it would seem.' It was laconic, but as the waiter chose that moment to bring the bill the moment passed without further comment.

It had turned much colder by the time they left the restaurant, the English weather as mercurial as always. Frost was already coating the pavements as Carter helped her into the cab he had ordered before they'd left the warm womb of the building, and she shivered as he joined her on the back seat. 'Cold?' He didn't wait for an answer, putting his arm round her and pulling her into him and almost immediately his mouth closed over hers.

The kiss was everything she had hoped it would be. Desire stirred deep in her belly and rippled outwards, burning her skin and causing *frissons* of pleasure that had her clenching every muscle in an effort to stop herself trembling.

'What's the matter?' He must have sensed her reaction because the dark head raised and she looked into glittering eyes. 'Relax, damn it. I'm not about to take you in the back of a taxi.'

How dared he? She sat upright with a sharp jerk, her face blazing. 'Believe me, Carter, you wouldn't get the chance,' she bit out furiously. 'I don't know what sort of women you're used to wining and dining, but it would take more than a good meal and a bottle of wine to get me into bed.'

'Really?' He looked amused and unperturbed by her

rage, folding his arms and surveying her with expression-less eyes. 'What would it take then?'

'More than you've got,' she shot back nastily.

'Is that a challenge?' he asked silkily.

She wasn't fooled by the lazy tone; she'd seen the grey eyes turn to hard stone. 'It's a statement.'

'A statement,' he repeated thoughtfully, raising his hand and stroking a lock of errant hair off her cheek. 'You're very flushed,' he drawled slowly. 'Warm and soft and de-liciously pink.'

He made her sound like a marshmallow. She fought the weakening desire the smoky voice was bringing forth with the thought. She wasn't going to fall for this; she was *not*.

'And kissable.' The gleam in his eyes darkened as he drew nearer and once again she was held in his embrace, but this time the kiss deepened immediately to a deter-mined seduction of her defences. Within a minute or two he had scaled every one. He was kissing her so thoroughly, so wonderfully, that resistance was the last thing on her mind as she kissed him back, her enthusiasm not quite hiding her lack of expertise.

By the time the cab drew into her street she was a quiv-ering wreck, utterly lost in the smell and feel of him and the sensations he had called forth so powerfully.

When the cab stopped outside her house and Carter raised his head it took Liberty a full ten seconds to stir herself, and then she felt as though her legs wouldn't hold her. 'A statement.' He murmured the words next to her mouth in the moment before he opened the cab door, and they were husky with the same desire which had gripped her. 'Care to rethink it?'

It took a second or two, but then she felt as though a bucket of cold water had been thrown in her face. He had been playing with her just now, proving a point. She ignored his outstretched hand and struggled out of the cab by herself, her face flaming. Of all the rotten, low down, manipulating…

'Careful.' The smoky tones were definitely amused now as she nearly landed on her bottom when her foot slid on the frosty pavement. 'We don't want to spoil a wonderful evening, do we?'

Conscious of the taxi driver, Liberty bit back the hot words hovering on her tongue, jerking his hand away from her elbow as she said, 'I can manage perfectly well, thank you. Goodnight, Carter, and thank you for a lovely meal.'

'I'll see you to your door,' he said lazily.

'There's no need.' She'd sooner be escorted by Dracula.

'On the contrary, with those heels and this frost there is every need.'

She wasn't going to prolong this farewell by arguing with him on the pavement. With as much dignity as she could muster, Liberty strode to the steps leading up to her front door, moderating her momentum when she found they were like sheets of glass. Once safely on her doorstep, she turned to Carter, who had paused on the step below. He was still taller than her, she realised, and much too close.

'Thank you and goodnight,' she said again, her tone matching the weather. That was the end of that, and a good job too.

'Goodnight, Liberty.' He seemed completely oblivious to her fury, but contrary to her expectations he didn't try for a last goodnight kiss, turning on his heel and disappearing back into the cab as she opened the front door. She had closed the door and put the lights on before she heard the cab draw away, and with its going she felt as though the wind had been taken out of her sails.

'Horrible man.' She stood in the middle of her sitting

room, her mind and body churning with so many emotions she couldn't have put a name to just one. And then, as she glared across the room, her gaze was caught and held by the vase of flowers on the coffee table and, to her absolute horror, she burst into tears.

# CHAPTER FOUR

IF ONLY she hadn't succumbed so completely. If only she had just allowed a goodnight kiss and that was all. But she had been putty in his hands and he had known it. Oh yes, he'd known it all right and had gloated over it too after her somewhat unwise words beforehand. She'd made such a mess of it all.

Liberty groaned with self-contempt for the umpteenth time that morning and flung the Sunday paper to one side, rising abruptly from the sofa and beginning to pace round the room before she restrained herself and sat down again. Calm, girl, calm. She tried a few breathing exercises she'd learnt during a yoga phase a few years before but nothing helped.

What had he thought? The answer was all too obvious and she groaned again, as she'd done throughout the long night when sleep had been a million miles away and she had dissected every word and action of the meal and the time in the cab in minute detail. He thought she said one thing and did another!

He hadn't suggested seeing her again. The thought which she had been keeping at bay with rigid will-power broke through at last. Not that she would have agreed, of course—she wouldn't, she most *definitely* wouldn't—but it would have been nice to be able to refuse nonetheless. Prick that giant ego just a bit.

As it was she was left with the most uncomfortable feeling that Carter had won hands down. She brushed her hair out of her face with irritable hands, rising abruptly and walking through to the bedroom where she combed it back into a high ponytail out of the way. She stared at herself in the mirror when she had finished. Tragic eyes stared back at her and she made a sound of exasperation at herself in her throat.

For goodness' sake, this wasn't the end of the world. Okay, so she'd made a bit of a fool of herself but she wasn't the first woman in the world to do that and she wouldn't be the last. Give it a couple of weeks and this would all be behind her and forgotten.

The thought mocked her but she ignored its ridiculousness and padded off to make herself a milky coffee. She was going to relax and enjoy her Sunday morning before she got on with some urgent work she had brought home. Then this evening she'd have a long perfumed bath with a glass of wine at the side of her and scented candles giving the bathroom a rosy glow, and then an early night so she was fresh and bright for Monday morning.

She cut herself a piece of coconut cake to have with the coffee, taking a slice out to the bird table and receiving due thanks from the resident robin before she went upstairs to the sitting room again. The brief contact with the little bird was cheering and she resolutely put all thoughts of Carter Blake out of her mind as she sat down and picked up the paper once more.

She hadn't read one word before a knock at the door brought her to her feet. She had long ago extended an open invitation to friends to drop by for a coffee if they were in her area on a Sunday morning, it being her only day of the week when she was sure she wouldn't be at the office. During the summer months almost every Sunday had seen her sitting in her tiny garden with someone or other, and often they would accompany her to her father's house for lunch, Mrs Harris always cooking enough to feed the five thousand. This week, however, she'd told her father she was likely to be working, purely to give him and Joan their first weekend together.

She pulled open the door, a smile on her face which faded into a little 'o' of shock as she took in Carter looking good enough to eat in jeans and a thick oatmeal sweater. 'Hi.' He seemed totally unaware of her surprise, acting as though she had expected him when he said, 'Is that coffee I can smell?'

'What…what are you doing here?'

Nothing in Carter's cool smile revealed that he had asked himself the same question. He had cancelled a long-standing lunch date and infuriated his golf partner by calling to say he couldn't make their afternoon round to come and see a woman who clearly wished him somewhere else. Now he lied through his back teeth as he said, 'I suddenly found myself at a loose end and wondered if you fancy lunch. I get maudlin if I eat alone.'

She eyed him suspiciously. He was the sort of man who could take or leave company; it was written all over him. She ignored the excitement which was causing her stomach to flutter with a thousand butterflies and said carefully, 'I was going to work this afternoon. I'm extremely busy at the moment.'

'You still can.' He raked back a lock of hair and her nerves responded with electricity. 'We needn't be late back.'

She was terribly conscious she hadn't got a scrap of make-up on and was wearing her oldest jeans and sweatshirt, and prayed her nose wasn't shiny. He had come to see her. *He wanted to see her again.* She swallowed. 'You'd better come in. Would you like a coffee?' she asked as she waved him through. 'I'm having one.'

'I'd love one.'

Immediately when he stepped into her little home it seemed to shrink and it made her even more all of a dither. She wasn't sure if she asked him to sit down or not, but when he followed her down the stairs to the kitchen she felt so nervous she almost dropped the coffee jar. 'It's just instant, I'm afraid.' She turned to face him as she spoke and then wished she hadn't as he was right behind her. And he was so very big.

'Instant's fine.' He didn't seem to notice her feverishness, perching himself on a kitchen stool and looking around appreciatively. 'This place feels like you.'

What did that mean? She wasn't at all sure if it was a compliment or not. She eyed him warily.

He caught her glance and startled her by throwing back his head and giving what could only be described as a belly laugh. 'Your home is unusual and beautiful with a touch of gracious quaintness,' he assured her solemnly but with his eyes still laughing. 'Tasteful and serene.'

Serene? If he thought she was serene he must be mad. Liberty stared at him, wondering how he managed to look taller, broader and altogether more mesmerising every time she saw him. 'Thank you.' She cleared her throat, aware that her voice had been little more than a croak. 'How do you take your coffee?'

'Hot and strong.' He eyed her wickedly. 'And I won't follow with the old line, like my women.'

She smiled; she couldn't help it.

'That's better.' He leaned forward, his face very close to hers and his grey eyes glinting. 'You know I like you, Miss Fox, and I think you could like me if you give it half a chance. We're very alike under the skin, you know.'

'We are?' she asked disbelievingly. And pigs could fly.

'Sure we are.' He'd sensed her incredulity, his voice reproving.

He slid off the stool and her senses went haywire. There had been a teasing note to his voice but his eyes were deadly serious as one finger stroked the outline of her mouth. She tried to remind herself how she had felt last night after his cold-blooded awakening of her desire in the cab to prove a point, but it didn't work. That had been then and this was now.

'You like honesty and truth in a relationship; so do I. You're not looking for a ring on your finger and vows of undying love; neither am I. Playing happy families with the requisite two point four kids is not on your agenda; it's not on mine. Need I go on? We could have fun together, you and I. I know it.'

His finger moved down her chin and traced a seductive path down her throat, her eyes widening as it stopped just inside her sweatshirt at the swell of her right breast. 'Carter—'

He stopped her going on by the simple expedient of placing his mouth on hers, pulling her into him so she was hard against his body. He kissed her thoroughly, so thoroughly she couldn't remember what she had wanted to say when he raised his head again. She tried to gather her scattered wits, her mind dazed.

'I like your soft, silky skin and your beautiful hair,' he said huskily. 'Do you know how many different colours it's got in it, the way it shines and shimmers when you move your head? And your eyes, deep and velvety, and...' He paused, his finger moving to her mouth again. 'And your lips. Warm, pouting, kissable lips. I especially like your lips.'

'The...the coffee.' She was out of her depth and she knew it. He was used to women who jumped in and out of bed without it meaning too much one way or the other beyond a brief sating of a bodily need and some fun. Experienced women.

'Damn the coffee,' he said throatily.

'No, Carter, listen. Please…' She pulled away from him, taking a step backwards as she said, 'I'm not… I don't—' She stopped abruptly, taking a deep breath to still the racing of her heart. 'I meant everything I said yesterday but that doesn't mean I go in for—' she had been about to say one night stands but changed it to '—affairs. I couldn't sleep with someone unless it means something.'

'Neither could I,' he said very softly.

Liberty was aware of a subtle electricity in the air, an almost tangible sense of expectation. She tried again. 'What I mean is—'

He stopped her with a raised hand. 'What you mean is that you like to take time to get to know someone,' he said quietly. 'Yes? And that's fine by me; I wouldn't have it any other way.'

'No. Yes.' She stopped, confused and bewildered by the suddenness with which her life had changed in just a few days.

Carter observed her in silence, waiting. When she had said the other day that she always slept alone, she hadn't meant… But no, it was impossible. Looking like she did there was no way she hadn't made love with a man before. Was there?

'My mother is at present being divorced by her fifth husband,' Liberty said with a flatness which spoke of iron control. 'He objected to her sleeping with his business associate which, to be fair, I can understand.' She gave a tight little smile. 'The business associate in question didn't run true to form however, and refused to leave his wife and children, which caused a hiccup in my mother's plans. She has always gone on to higher things, you understand.

My mother exercises for hours every day, spends a fortune on tightening this and tucking that, and yet has no respect for her body at all. Any man, depending on whether he has the right connections and a fat bank balance, of course, can buy her.'

For once in his life Carter didn't know what to say.

'I don't need a man in my life.' She raised shadowed eyes to his. 'I can survive perfectly well on my own and I like it that way. I'm sorry if I led you to think otherwise.'

'Do you hate her?' he said very quietly.

'What?' The starkness threw her completely.

'Your mother? Do you hate her for leaving you and adding to that sin by going from man to man?'

It was her fault, she'd told him it all, but hearing her life compounded into one harsh sentence was not easy. She felt the warm colour surge into her cheeks and wished she had never opened her mouth. But she had. And now he knew. 'I've tried to over the years,' she said after long seconds had ticked away. 'But she's my mother. No, I don't hate her.' She shrugged painfully. 'I love her but I don't like her one little bit.'

'Then why have you let her influence you rather than your dad?'

'What?' she said again, her eyes shooting up to meet his. 'I haven't, of course I haven't. I adore my father and he's a wonderful man. I've always listened to him.'

'I don't think so.' And before she could object he continued. 'By your own admission your mother is less than morally stable whereas your father is just the opposite. And yet you seem intent on judging men, marriage—life in general, in fact, by the disappointment and disenchantment you feel about her.'

Liberty felt a rage such as she hadn't experienced in

years rise up in her. 'You know nothing about it,' she bit out savagely. 'You don't know me or my parents.'

'True.' There was no expression at all in his voice. 'Which is why I am qualified to give a fair and unbiased observation. No messy emotional entanglement confusing the issue.'

If his coffee had been ready she would have thrown it at him. 'I would like you to leave now,' she said in a small, cold voice. 'And I would prefer you not to call again.'

'What I would like is to take your clothes off, look at you, stroke and touch you, kiss and caress you all over and make love to you until neither of us can move a muscle,' he returned coolly, 'so it looks as if neither of us is going to get what we want.'

Now it was Liberty who didn't know what to say. She stared at him, hurt beyond measure by some of the things he had said and yet wanting to break into hysterical laughter. She had never met anyone like him in the whole of her life. She made a helpless gesture with her hands just as the kettle announced it was boiling and switched itself off.

'Why don't I make myself a cup of coffee while you go and change ready for lunch?' Carter asked with magnificent matter-of-factness, for all the world as though they had been discussing the current cricket scores rather than the most intimate recesses of her heart. 'There's a pub just outside Harlow where the landlady makes a steak and kidney pie with pastry worth dying for, and the raspberry trifle has enough booze in it to make it a driving hazard.'

For a moment he thought she was going to refuse and tell him to get out again, but after a long moment she merely nodded, her mouth tremulous as she turned and left the room.

Carter made the coffee strong and black and reseated

himself on the stool. For someone who gave an outward persona of cool self-control and independence, she was appallingly vulnerable. There was a fragility about her, a diffidence, which was all the more surprising considering the sort of job she held down. A woman of contrasts. He narrowed his eyes reflectively. And he had only just touched the surface yet.

Was it fair to continue with this, knowing he had no intention of it leading to more than an enjoyable interlude for both of them? He looked down at his shoes, considering. But he'd spelt it out and she knew where she stood, as did he. Besides which—his innate honesty kicked in—he could no more walk away from her right now than fly to the moon. She'd got under his skin. He didn't know quite when it had happened in the last few days, but happen it had.

It had been years since he had indulged in erotic fantasies, but since he had met Liberty Fox she had invaded his mind when he had been asleep and awake. And he didn't like that. He frowned in the small bright room. He didn't like that at all. So the answer was to get her out of his system. Simple.

He relaxed on the stool, satisfied he had dealt with the problem logically. He would take it at her pace; he was in no hurry, after all—he ignored the burning in his loins which the feel of her body pressed against his had induced and which was taking a while to die down—and just see how things went. That was what he'd do.

He finished the coffee in one gulp, washed up the cup and dried it with a tea towel which stated that Cornwall's beaches were the best in the world. Then he went upstairs to wait for her.

\*    \*    \*

Carter hadn't exaggerated about the food. The pub was all brass and oak beams with a huge log fire—as befitted a building boasting to be over three hundred years old—and every morsel of the delicious dinner tasted heavenly.

Too many dates with Carter, Liberty reflected, and she would resemble a fat little balloon. With this in mind, she said, 'How is it you know of so many good places to eat, anyway?'

Carter leant back in his seat, smiling at her. 'I've only taken you to two yet,' he reminded her lazily. 'There's a lot to go.'

She flushed slightly. She still didn't know if she wanted to date this man. She had the feeling that once Carter Blake had established himself in your life the hole which would be left when he departed would be unfillable.

'I've always considered eating one of the main pleasures of life,' he went on, as though he hadn't noticed her withdrawal. 'Not *the* main one, of course—' the grey eyes glinted wickedly but she refused to blush any further '—but very pleasant, nevertheless. Maybe it's because when I was a youngster we were fed on anything cheap and filling. My mother always made sure we didn't go to bed hungry, bless her, so we were a lot better off than some, but boiled potatoes, bread and stodgy batter pudding pall after a time.' It was said without any self-consciousness or self-pity, merely a statement of fact.

'But you didn't want to be a chef like Adam?'

'Hell, no.' He gave her a slow grin. 'Can you see me in a long hat and a pinny?'

'They're called aprons,' she corrected, smiling.

'Whatever.' He straightened, finishing his coffee before he said, 'That's the guy Jen should have married, you know.'

'Adam?' She stared at him in surprise.

'They've always had that certain something between them right from kids; some people do.' The heavily lashed eyes moved over her face for a moment and for some reason Liberty felt a little flutter of trepidation, almost fear.

'What happened to them?' she asked carefully, telling herself he'd meant nothing by that remark other than what he'd said. He'd already said he wasn't interested in commitment and for ever, hadn't he?

Carter shrugged. 'I'm not sure; life, I guess. Jen went away to university and Adam got involved in courses for catering, working unsocial hours once he'd qualified and then even more so when he decided to go for his own business. Jen would bring the odd boyfriend back and he'd respond by dating someone—' He broke off, his voice holding a note of irritation when he said, 'Silly games. Games which got out of hand.'

'And then she married someone else.'

He nodded. 'After that Adam went through a time of dating everything in a skirt and drinking too much, although he'd rather cut his own throat than admit he missed the boat with Jen. Crazy thing, human nature.'

Liberty suppressed a wry smile. If Adam had a large dose of male pride she suspected Carter had it by the lorry load. 'But now your sister is divorced there's a chance for him, isn't there?' she suggested. 'If they both still like each other?'

'If they can get their act together,' he said dryly. 'Up to now Adam's made no move and neither has she. Still, they'll have to meet at the party I'm throwing for my parents for their fortieth wedding anniversary next month. You're invited,' he added casually. 'Make sure you keep that weekend free.'

She threw him a blank look before recovering enough to say, 'To your parents' party? But they don't know me;

I wouldn't want to intrude.' She'd feel like a fish out of water, for sure.

'You will be with me so there will be no question of intruding,' he said with faint emphasis.

Liberty didn't know what to say. She had the feeling things were moving much too fast and out of her control. 'Thank you,' she said at last. 'If I don't have to work I would love to come.' And she'd make sure something urgent cropped up.

The get-out clause. Carter's eyelids lowered momentarily, hiding the flicker of anger she might have read in his eyes. 'Fine,' he said lazily, pouring them both another coffee from the pot the landlady of the pub had left on their table. 'There's plenty of time to let me know because it's not till the twentieth.'

She nodded, relieved he didn't seem to care one way or the other and suppressing the dart of pique that accompanied the relief. What was the matter with her? she asked herself silently. She couldn't have her cake and eat it. She didn't want to get heavily involved with this man, so there was no reason to resent the fact that he could take her or leave her.

They continued to talk about this and that but now the conversation progressed down safer channels. She told him all about acquiring her little house and the changes she had made, and he in turn related how he had turned a disused asphalt factory near Notting Hill into a state-of-the-art, four-bedroom minimalist home. 'Come and see it,' he suggested blandly as they rose to leave the pub. 'Jen's out to lunch with a couple of friends but she might be back by now.'

She knew she ought to refuse. One, it would confirm—at least to her—that she was in control of the situation and this disturbing man. Two, she really did have some work to do at home. Three, it would be giving all the wrong signals to agree to go back to his home; it would suggest she was curious about him and wanted to know more. Which she did. Liberty blinked. And she was probably going to be hanged by the old adage that curiosity killed the cat, but she just couldn't *help* it.

'Just a quick visit, then,' she said weakly as he took her arm, guiding her through a crowd of young people who had just come in and were filling the bar area with walking boots and hiking gear. 'I really do have to work later.'

'All work and no play…'

'Oh, I play.' She was stung into retaliating to his murmur as they stepped into the cold October air and began to walk towards the Mercedes, the scratches on the paintwork reproaching her. 'Of course I play when time permits.'

'I'm very pleased to hear it,' he said soothingly, in a tone which irritatingly reeked of disbelief.

Liberty decided dignified silence was the best put-down.

By the time they drew up outside the large square building which was Carter's home, Liberty had prepared herself for what she might see. Nevertheless, she was still unnerved by the reality of the size of the building. With the cost of accommodation per square foot so expensive in London, the awareness of Carter's wealth was a little daunting.

Towering metal gates set in a high wall at the side of the building were opened by Carter from remote control within the vehicle. When the Mercedes had purred through, Liberty found herself in a large paved area with a square holding a fountain surrounded by seats and tables at the side of her and a block of garages in front. An enormous barbecue ran the length of one wall.

They entered the building by means of an impressive

arched wooden door and immediately the mellow maple
flooring and sweeping cantilevered staircase spoke of
space and light. Carter led the way into a massive lounge,
one wall of which consisted almost entirely of floor to
ceiling windows with a small area of brick between. The
pale wood floor, curtains and furnishings in biscuit, cream
and coffee were impressive and dramatic—the ultimate
bachelor pad, Liberty thought wryly. And Carter was the
ultimate bachelor.

'Doesn't look like Jen's back yet.' Carter helped her off
with her coat, throwing it with his onto one of the two-
seater sofas dotted about the vast room before he said,
'Come and see the rest of it and tell me what you think.'

The rest of it comprised of a dining room, kitchen and
utility room and a study on the ground floor, three guest
bedrooms all with *en suite* bathrooms and a master bedroom complete with a moulded marble terrazzo bath big
enough for two on the first floor, and a swimming pool,
steam room and gym in the basement.

All the walls shimmered with the elegant finish of white
Italian marmorino plasterwork; there was no clutter, no
knick-knacks and no fuss, just cool architectural perfec-
tion. Liberty couldn't rid herself of the impression she was
in a luxurious and coldly beautiful hotel, and this was
heightened by the fact that music, television, security,
room temperature and lighting were all controlled from
one neat handheld console in each room. This was definitely not the house of a prospective family man.

She made appropriate noises of interest and appreciation
as the tour progressed, swallowing hard at the charcoal and
cream master bedroom with its mirrored ceiling, suspended
television and DVD screen, below which a huge bed of
indecent proportions lay, but when they walked into the
lounge again she realised the whole house gave no clue to

the real Carter whatsoever. And she felt that was intentional.

'You don't like it.'

It was a statement, not a question, but Liberty responded as if to the latter. 'Of course I like it,' she said quickly. 'How could anyone not like such a beautiful house?'

He smiled, his hand reaching up to stroke her hair. 'Little liar,' he said softly. 'I don't mind if you don't like it; Jen doesn't, as it happens.'

'I do like it,' she argued, 'but—'

'What?' He was eyeing her with amusement now.

'It's not… Oh, I don't know, homely enough for me, I suppose. But it is beautiful.'

He lifted her chin, looking deep into the brown velvet of her eyes before he kissed her. She could feel the strong, solid beating of his heart as he held her against his chest, the warm scent of him all about her. 'There wasn't enough room to swing a cat at home when I was young,' he said softly, raising his head so that his chin was resting on the silk of her hair. 'I guess this house is a backlash from that.'

'I've never wanted to swing a cat,' she said just as softly, aiming to break the suddenly elusive but strangely intimate atmosphere which had sprung up when he had taken her into his arms.

'Wise girl.' She couldn't see his face but there was no laughter in his voice. But then he had lowered his head again and talk wasn't necessary.

His mouth was sure of what it wanted and as it kindled the aching passion she had felt before in his arms, Liberty surrendered to its authority. Sensation was trickling to all parts of her body as his lips continued to search and explore, warm desire holding her in another world where only the senses of touch and taste and smell mattered.

His fingers had slipped under the light top she was wearing, moving up to stroke the back of her neck in caressing movements which caused a heat beneath his touch.

Her breathing was slow and heavy and she could hear the little moans she was uttering but was unable to stem the flow. Her breasts were tight and sharp as his fingers moved in a circular movement to cup their fullness. She had never felt this need with anyone else, her mind was saying in dazed wonder, not even with Gerard, who had been an accomplished lover. This was... Her mind searched for a suitable description but the pleasure her body was experiencing took over.

It was a drenching shock when, in the next moment, a woman's voice called out, 'Carter? I'm back and the lunch was foul. I'm going to—'

Liberty had jerked away at the first word, adjusting her clothes and smoothing her hair, so when Jennifer appeared in the doorway it was her brother's glare which cut off her voice rather than any visual embarrassment.

'Hello, Jen.' Carter was the first to recover, his voice cool as he smoothed his face clear of all expression. 'This is Liberty. Liberty, meet Jen.'

'Oh, I'm sorry.' Jennifer was too taken aback to be tactful. 'I didn't realise... I mean—'

'I think we know what you mean,' said Carter, a corner of his mouth slanting up. 'Say hello nicely.'

'Hello.' Jennifer held out her hand to Liberty after one quick sisterly sticking out of her tongue at Carter. 'We spoke the other day on the phone, didn't we?'

'That's right.' Just two days ago, to be exact, and since then she and Carter had progressed to—Liberty didn't like to think what they had progressed to.

'I hope your lunch was better than mine.' Jennifer wrinkled her small snub nose. 'Everything was stone cold, the meat was tough and the potatoes were as hard as iron.'

'Bad luck.' Carter clearly couldn't care less.

'Would you like some coffee?' Jennifer ignored her brother and spoke directly to Liberty. 'I'm going to make some along with a couple of rounds of toasted sandwiches.'

'Thanks, but I really do have to be going.'

'Oh, don't go.' Carter's sister stretched out her hand, her voice sounding as though she meant it when she said, 'I've been dying to meet the woman who's made such an impact on my brother.'

'It wasn't such an impact,' Carter interjected coolly, 'just a few scratches on the paintwork.'

Liberty was barely listening. She hadn't felt so embarrassed since Miss Finn, the art teacher, had caught her canoodling with Dean Miller behind the bike sheds in the fifth form. Loads of couples had kissed and carried on behind the bike sheds every day of every week, but the first time she had been persuaded to go there she'd been hauled up before the Head as though it was the crime of the century, despite the fact that their tentative kisses had hardly been kisses at all. She couldn't remember exactly what the Head had said—time had blunted the edges—but there had been some reference to her mother in a way which had let her know the Head knew all about her mother's men. It had been enough to ensure she hadn't kissed another boy for years.

'I'm sorry, but I really do have to go,' Liberty said now, smiling at Carter's sister and hoping she wasn't as flushed as she felt. 'I've some urgent work to do for a meeting first thing tomorrow morning. Carter's just finished showing me round the house.'

'Sterile, isn't it?' Jennifer was small and pretty with a dimple that flashed as she said, 'Full of boy's toys with all the gadgets and things, but I've hopes he'll grow up yet.'

'Say goodbye, Jen.'

Jennifer's sidelong glance at her brother must have convinced her she had gone far enough because her voice was meek when she said, 'Goodbye, Liberty. It was nice to meet you.'

'Goodbye.'

Not much was said until they were on their way again, but as they left Notting Hill, Liberty proffered, 'She's nice, your sister.'

'Not a word that comes to my mind when I think of Jen,' Carter said evenly. 'Not today, anyway.'

Liberty swallowed hard. 'I hope she didn't think…' She found she didn't know quite how to put it.

'That I was kissing you? But I was.'

There were kisses and then there were kisses. Grandmothers kissed grandchildren. Friends kissed socially. 'You know what I mean,' she said weakly.

Carter arched an eyebrow. 'Do I?'

Hateful man. She didn't deign to answer.

'Liberty, why does it matter one jot what Jen thinks?' Carter asked very calmly. 'We're seeing each other; she wouldn't expect we refrain from any bodily contact.'

They were seeing each other? When had that been decided? She took a deep breath. 'Look, Carter—'

'We *are* seeing each other, Liberty.' His voice brooked no argument. 'I accept that very intelligent mind of yours has probably put up a hundred and one arguments why that shouldn't happen, but it is happening, take it from me. I want to see you and you want to see me. It's really very simple.'

She didn't believe this. The arrogance of the man. Liberty tried to work up the rage and resentment she felt she should be experiencing but it just wasn't there. She *did* want to see Carter. She wanted it so much it was a physical pain, but it was dangerous, and she wasn't the sort of woman who flirted with danger.

'I won't ask you for more than you feel you want to give,' he continued steadily, his eyes on the road ahead and his profile expressionless. 'Either physically or emotionally. We'll take it at your pace, okay?'

'As friends?' she asked tentatively after a few moments.

'*Friends?*' There was a note of disbelief in his voice. 'Honey, I have to tell you in case you haven't already guessed, but the feelings I have for you don't come under the heading of friend. Adam's a friend, okay? And a good one. You're something else.' He flashed a quick glance at her pink face.

She smiled; she couldn't help it. His voice had been so wry.

'Okay, not exactly friends,' she compromised after a moment. 'But I don't want anything heavy, Carter. Not in any way. I'm not ready for that.'

He gave her one swift, searching look and then turned back to the road ahead. 'I might have a good few things on my conscience,' he said evenly, 'but forcing a woman is not one of them. If this fizzles out like a damp squib, so be it. If not...' He shrugged. 'We take it a day at a time. How's that?'

She couldn't answer, couldn't speak for a moment. It ought to be fine, of course it ought—it was more than reasonable, all things considered. So then why did she feel so odd, so afraid? She shook herself mentally, angry with her weakness but unable to do anything about it. 'That's fine,' she said at last because the atmosphere was tensing and stretching. 'A day at a time.'

# CHAPTER FIVE

LIBERTY couldn't honestly have said that the next three weeks weren't the best of her life because they were.

She and Carter saw each other every single evening and the odd lunchtime too, until Liberty found herself wondering what she'd done with her time before Carter filled it to the hilt. But life before him was now just a vague memory.

He took her out to the theatre, the cinema, art galleries and restaurants, but they also went for long walks when they talked and laughed and discussed everything under the sun. Almost. If the subject turned to her mother Liberty wouldn't be drawn. The things he'd said before still burnt in her mind.

She cooked dinner for Carter a couple of times in her little home, and they dined with Jennifer at Carter's palatial establishment too. The more Liberty got to know Carter's sister the more she liked her, and when the other woman asked Liberty to meet her one lunchtime to go and look at a flat that Jennifer was interested in, Liberty agreed at once.

'It's no good asking Carter,' Jennifer said, wrinkling her nose as she was apt to do when making a point. 'His taste is so not mine it isn't true. His ideal place would be bare rooms with everything appearing out of the floor and walls when he pressed a button. Sterile, controlled and empty.'

'A slight exaggeration,' Carter drawled lazily, 'but once you find somewhere that suits I'll send Peter to have a look at it before you go any further.'

'Carter's surveyor friend,' Jennifer explained in an aside to Liberty as she helped herself to another helping of cheesecake. 'Carter has a contact for absolutely every eventuality, don't you, Carter? Bit frightening when you think about it.'

Carter surveyed his sister over the top of his wineglass. 'I like to keep my finger on the pulse,' he said mildly.

The two women went to look at the two-bedroom, first-floor apartment in Knightsbridge the next day. It was bright and warm with magnificent views over the communal gardens, and as it was set in an attractive purpose-built block the security was good. There was something institutional about it, however.

After Jennifer had told the estate agent she would let him know whether she was going to put in an offer by the next morning, she treated Liberty to lunch at a little bistro. Once they had ordered, Carter's sister leant forward, her elbows on the table, and said, 'He's mad about you. You know that, don't you? Absolutely mad. I've never seen him like this before.'

Liberty had got used to Jennifer's frankness over the last weeks but even so she was a little taken aback. She didn't prevaricate, however, merely smiling as she said, 'I like him too,' hoping that would end the conversation.

Jennifer's blue eyes closed momentarily. 'Liberty, you *like* a film or a book or chocolate cake,' she said exasperatedly. 'Or me, come to that.'

Liberty wasn't quite sure about that right at this moment.

'But you don't *like* a man like Carter. That's too—' she searched for the right word '—too *weak* a word. You either adore him or loathe him, he's that sort of guy.'

Liberty took a sip of her mineral water. She had an important case on that afternoon and needed a clear head so had refused to accompany Jennifer in a glass of wine. 'I'm seeing him so I don't loathe him,' she said coolly, not liking the way the conversation was going. 'Okay?'

'Oh, don't freeze me out.' In her spontaneous way, Jennifer reached across and squeezed Liberty's arm. 'I'm only saying this for your own good. If you do feel something special for him, for goodness' sake let him know, that's all. Learn by my mistake.'

'Your mistake?' Liberty asked carefully.

'With Adam.' Jennifer relaxed back in her seat, frowning slightly. 'I always thought we'd be together when I was younger and I know he liked me then. But I went away to university and he didn't bother to come and see me or write or anything. I felt he was…sort of ignoring me, I suppose.'

'Wasn't he doing a course himself and working at night to pay for it?' Carter had related this bit so she knew it was true. Adam had nearly driven himself into the ground at the time.

Jennifer nodded, her mouth turning down at the edges. 'I didn't really take that into account, I guess. I know that now, but I was younger then and… Oh, I don't know. Anyway, I thought I'd try and make him jealous so he'd buck up his ideas.'

'But it didn't work?' She didn't reveal that she knew it hadn't.

Jennifer shook her head dolefully. 'He went out with other girls and things got all strained and horrible. He didn't want to know any more.'

'I'm sure that's not true. He was probably feeling hurt.'

'Even on the morning I was getting married I thought of him.' Jennifer looked across the table, her eyes bleak. 'But then there was this other guy who thought I was all his Christmases rolled up in one—or so I thought at the time,' she added with a touch of bitterness. 'Anyway, that's all history.' She straightened. 'What I'm saying is, if I'd said something to Adam at least I'd have known one way or the other how he felt. Now I'll always wonder but it's too late. I just wouldn't want the same thing to happen to you. Especially not with my own brother. I do care about him, you know.'

'But that's just it, Jen,' Liberty said gently. 'He *is* your brother, which colours how you see things. But I'll bear in mind what you've said, I promise.'

'You *will* be coming to Mum and Dad's party, won't you?' Jennifer did the wrinkling of the nose thing. 'Adam's bound to turn up with one of his model type girlfriends and it'd just be nice to have someone in my corner. I've never discussed this with Carter, him being Adam's best friend, but I think he'd feel I got exactly what I deserve.'

'Course he wouldn't.' Liberty thought it prudent not to mention Carter was fully aware of the situation.

'But you will come?' Jennifer persisted. '*Please*, Libby.'

Liberty nodded. She didn't want to go and it was only in this moment that she admitted she had been going to pull out at the last minute and use work as an excuse. The party was being held in a hotel close to Carter's parents' home, which would necessitate an overnight stay, but it wasn't that which was causing her to feel apprehensive. The thought of meeting his parents, of being there with all his relations and so on was overwhelming. She didn't want to see him as dutiful son and nephew and what have you; it was too cosy, too tempting. She needed to keep him in the little box in her head labelled Man about town and ladies' man. Then she could cope.

Once back at work she sat at her desk, staring at the papers in front of her without really seeing them. The conversation at lunch had bothered her more than she liked, she admitted silently, and the very thing she should be pleased about—that Carter hadn't put a foot wrong over the last little while—was niggling at her incessantly.

She wanted to find some things about him she didn't like. She sighed irritably. If he had made it obvious he wanted her in bed or else their relationship was over, if he'd been pushy or awkward or difficult it would be easier to keep him at arm's length, at least in her head where it mattered. But he had been—perfect was the word which came to mind but she changed it to—great. Much, much too great, in fact.

Was she in love with him? The question which had been hammering at her mind since the conversation with Jennifer wouldn't be ignored any longer. She raised bleak eyes. No, she was not. She would not let herself be. To fall for a man like Carter, a self-confessed love-em and leave-em type, would be the height of stupidity. And she wasn't stupid. Far from it. They'd had fun, admittedly, but that was all it was.

Her chin rose aggressively. This Saturday it was the party—three days away—and she would keep her promise to Jennifer and be there. But once she was home again she would put a brake on this crazy relationship. If she was truthful she knew there had been several times lately when it had been Carter who had called a halt to their lovemaking before things went too far—not her. She frowned. He was just too good at it, that was the trouble. Too experienced, too knowledgeable about which buttons to press at any given moment.

But it wasn't just that. Her gaze fell to the papers again and she knew she should get working on them, but still her mind chugged remorselessly on.

It was getting—no, it had got—so that she needed Carter

in her life. She took a hard pull of air, brushing back her hair with a shaky hand. And she didn't want to need anyone. It wasn't what she had planned for her life. The turbulence of her mother's relationships over the years had both saddened and faintly disgusted her—so many complicated threads, so much disappointment, betrayal and cruelty. Her work she understood. Her home was under her control. No nasty surprises. No cringe-inducing scenes. No embarrassment and shame.

Whatever she wanted in life she would get for herself, unlike her mother. She didn't want to play the games men and women played where only one could win and the loser was in danger of losing even their self-respect. Nothing, and no one, was worth that.

'I'm sorry to bother you, Miss Fox, but Mr Cassell wondered if he might have a word before the meeting.'

Her secretary's voice was quiet and respectful as it came through on the intercom between the main office and her own small one. Only the senior partners had their secretaries ensconced in splendid isolation in adjoining rooms.

'Now?' Liberty asked evenly.

'Yes, Miss Fox. I understand he's waiting for you.'

'I'll be there directly.' Now this she understood. The ground rules and the hierarchy, the system in which status and authority ranked, was all perfectly clear here. No confusion or doubt, no nail-biting post mortems or breathless questioning of her own self.

She sat for a moment more, her face pale and her hands joined together as her fingers worked at each other. But then she rose to her feet, wiping her face clear of all expression as she gathered together the papers in front of her preparatory to walking through to Mr Cassell's office.

She would make it clear to Carter that their brief liaison was over right after the party, and she would cancel their

dinner engagement tonight, saying she had to work late.
And she should work late if it came to that. She had been
neglecting things the last two or three weeks and one
didn't aspire to senior management doing that.

Her throat muscles began to contract but she swallowed
hard, refusing to acknowledge any distress. It was over,
but in a way it had never begun.


Carter stared at the telephone and uttered an expletive with
such force it seemed to echo round the confines of his
study. She had to work. Twice running. Who was kidding
who here? Last night he could buy the tale of an urgent
case even though he had thought she seemed odd, remote,
but tonight he knew he hadn't been imagining the coolness
in her voice. Did she still intend to travel to the coast with
him tomorrow? She had said so but, as things were going,
who knew?

He rose to his feet, striding across to the study window
and glaring out into the darkness beyond. He'd booked a
table at Adam's place for eight; he had better ring and say
it wasn't needed.

His hands were halfway through dialling the number
when he replaced the telephone. Damn it, he was hungry.
He couldn't force Liberty to accompany him but there was
no reason he couldn't go himself. He was blowed if he
was going to sit at home twiddling his thumbs while his
stomach rolled.

An hour later he left the house and drove far too fast to
the restaurant, earning himself a flash from one of the
speed cameras *en route*, which didn't improve his dispo-
sition. Adam appeared from the kitchens a minute or so
after he had grimly informed the waiter that he was dining
alone, and Carter watched his friend seat himself in the

vacant chair opposite him. 'Problem?' Adam enquired mildly.

Carter shrugged. 'She's working late.'

'And?'

'And nothing. She's working late.'

'Okay, okay, don't bite my head off.'

Carter glanced at this friend who was the brother he'd never had. 'Shouldn't you be in the kitchens doing whatever it is that you do?' he asked ungraciously.

Adam stretched out his long legs and smiled. 'I've taken on a new chef,' he said contentedly, 'now the business can afford it. Takes the pressure off me a bit and means I can enjoy the odd weekend away, like this weekend, for instance. Thought I'd stay over Saturday night. What do you think?'

'Right,' said Carter.

'Hey, cut the enthusiasm, it's overwhelming.'

'You taking my order?' Carter asked grimly.

'Sure.' Adam rose to his feet. 'The usual?'

'No.' Carter glared at him. 'I'll have mange-tout and spring onion with serrano ham followed by cod with lemon and herbed potatoes.'

Adam stared at him. 'You don't like cod. You always say it's not fishy enough.' As black brows beetled together, Adam said hastily, 'Okay, cod it is,' and disappeared into the back.

Maybe it was just as well Liberty was bowing out, if that was what she was doing, Carter told himself morosely. She spelt danger. He had known it four weeks ago when he had first set eyes on her; he just hadn't admitted it to himself then. He wanted her as he'd never wanted a woman and he hadn't had a decent night's sleep since he'd met her.

Damn it, she had turned his world upside down and no

one did that, not to him. Was he going crazy? Yeah, he answered himself. Crazy with lust. That was all it was—good old-fashioned animal lust.

Then why, the voice outside himself asked, haven't you bedded her and be done with it? You could have, you know you could have. She's been putty in your hands more than once.

Because it wasn't like that, *she* wasn't like that. If he'd just wanted sexual intimacy, any one of a number of women he knew would do, but with Liberty… He raked his hand through his hair, groaning silently as he tried to feel his way through a whole host of emotions he hadn't wanted to face for days. With Liberty he wanted more. After all his macho words, he wanted more. Real intimacy. Physical, mental and emotional. The sort of intimacy his parents had. The sort that lasted a lifetime.

His grim face persuaded the waiter to put his mange-tout and spring onion with serrano ham in front of the customer without a word and make a hasty retreat.

He had thought they were doing fine. Making real progress. So what had happened? Why had she gone cold on him?

He munched his way through his first and second course and the excellent caramelised spiced apples with rosemary which followed without tasting much of anything, but by the time Adam judged it safe to come out again and sit down at the table Carter had come to a decision. He glared at Adam.

'I'm not going to roll over and play dead,' he announced grimly. 'I'm damned if I will.'

'You're not?' Adam glanced at the bottle on the table but as far as he could see it was only sparkling mineral water.

'And I'm blowed if I'm going to let her ruin something

which has the potential to get better and better. I don't care what this mother of hers has got up to but she has to see she's different. *We're* different.'

'Quite so.' Adam nodded encouragingly; it seemed safer.

'If she wants a fight, I'll give her a fight, but there will be two winners.'

Adam had given up. 'Isn't there always?'

'So you agree with me?'

'Totally.'

'Male logic, you see.' Carter nodded to himself. 'Apply a bit of male logic and it's sorted.' He stood up, pressing some notes into Adam's hand as he said, 'Great meal and thanks for the chat.'

'Think nothing of it.'

Adam was still standing staring after him a full minute after Carter had left.

# CHAPTER SIX

LIBERTY hadn't known quite how Carter would be when he arrived to pick her up after work on Friday evening. She wasn't looking forward to the drive to Great Yarmouth where his parents lived, but had taken comfort in the fact that Jennifer would be in the car too. It had been arranged that the three of them would meet Carter's parents for an evening meal at the hotel where the party was being held the next day, and Carter had wanted to arrive with enough time for the three of them to freshen up and change before his parents arrived.

Liberty had left work early so she would be ready when Carter arrived just before five o'clock, and when she heard the doorbell ring she had to take several deep breaths to calm her racing pulse. It didn't work.

'Hi, stranger.' As she opened the door he moved past her without waiting for an invitation, turning to face her once he was in the sitting room and taking her into his arms before she could object. He kissed her long and hard and she found herself responding to the hunger with a yearning which was all at odds with what she had decided. After a while Carter lifted his head, putting her away from him a little as he said, 'Boy, I needed that. I haven't had a fix for three days, after all. How's the workload?' he asked casually. 'Better?'

She stared at his smiling face, her legs trembling a little and feeling as though the strength had drained from her body. She had thought he might be aloof, cool, even angry, but he was behaving as though everything was just the

same between them. Had he really taken her excuses of
working late at face value, or was this some kind of act?

'The workload?' he prompted again, his voice gentle,
when she continued to stare at him.

She tried to pull herself together. 'Still chaotic,' she said
quickly. 'Everyone's working flat out at the moment.'

'Jennifer is pleased you've made time to come this
weekend.' He reached for her again, wrapping her up in
his arms as he said over her head, 'As am I, of course.'

'It was difficult,' she murmured faintly, the feel and delicious smell of him making her want to cling to him and
beg him to never let her go. She felt confused and all at
sea and she wanted to weep. 'But I promised Jen.'

*She loved him.* Useless to tell herself she didn't because
she did. Against everything she had told herself since she
had met him, all the good and intelligent arguments she
had put forth, she had gone and fallen in love with him.
Stupid, stupid, stupid. She should never have got involved
with him.

'So, all ready?' Carter said cheerfully.

As he drew away again she wasn't quite quick enough
to clear her face of all expression, but if he noticed her
tragic eyes he made no comment.

She nodded wordlessly, not trusting herself to speak
right at that moment but pointing to her case standing by
the door with her coat draped over it.

Once they were in the car, Jennifer's effusive greeting
and animated chatter helped establish something of a normal atmosphere, but Liberty found she was painfully aware
of every tiny movement Carter made at the side of her. He
was dressed in immaculate charcoal trousers and an open-
necked grey shirt, his jacket and tie lying on the back seat
next to Jennifer, and he rolled up the sleeves of the shirt
just before they started on their way. The dark hair on his

forearms as his hands held the wheel and the way the trousers pulled tight over hard, powerful male thighs kept his virile masculinity very much to the forefront of Liberty's mind, however much she tried to concentrate on the view through the windscreen.

Did he know how much she wanted him? Did he have any idea how often she lay awake at night with her body burning and restless as she imagined the hairy roughness of his naked flesh on hers, his hands and mouth touching her, caressing her, tasting her all over until their mingled pleasure reached a climactic crescendo? She hoped not. Oh, she did so hope not. Her heart began beating extra fast and the blood rushed up to her ears. How was she going to get through this weekend? How was she going to get through the rest of her *life*?

The Mercedes ate up the miles to the coast with comfort and ease once they were out of the bottleneck of London, and they arrived at the hotel with twenty minutes to spare before they met Carter's parents in the cocktail lounge at half past eight. It was the last word in luxury. As Carter talked to one of the women on reception, Liberty and Jennifer gazed round the plush surroundings.

The manager himself appeared to show them to their rooms, a gangling bellboy in a smart uniform accompanying him and taking the women's cases, although Carter insisted he would carry his own. As Liberty listened to the manager's somewhat obsequious chatter she found herself wondering if Carter liked that sort of thing.

She didn't know, she thought suddenly. Although the last weeks had been so intense, with barely a minute of spare time spent other than with Carter, what did she *really* know about him? Only the image he had projected. That was it in a nutshell. Of course it might be an honest and true picture but she had no way of knowing that for sure.

But then men and women who had known their partners for years sometimes had nasty surprises. She supposed it all came down to trust in the end, but she didn't think she was capable of trusting that a relationship with a member of the opposite sex would ever stand the test of time.

She was doing the right thing in ending this after the weekend. She'd had the caution light turn from amber to red, flashing the danger signal bright and clear. If she didn't retreat now, she would get so mired down in this relationship she wouldn't be able to see the wood for the trees, and there would be no hope of extricating her heart whole when things went wrong. She ignored the fact it was too late already.

From his viewpoint over the manager's balding head Carter was aware of every fleeting expression on Liberty's face. He felt a renewal of the determination which had been with him since the night before in Adam's restaurant, despite his heart feeling as though it was being squeezed by a giant hand. Only the memory of how she had responded to him in her home earlier, that and the fact that he knew they'd shared something special which had been growing steadily in depth and intensity over the last weeks, persuaded him he would make her see reason. To give up now would ruin both their lives.

This unfamiliar and penetrating emotion that was so much more than merely desire frightened him too, he reflected grimly. She wasn't the only one. But the thought of having to do without her scared him more.

The lift stopped at the second floor, which was also the top floor of the hotel, and the manager bowed them out before scuttling past Carter to open a door halfway down the hushed and scented corridor. 'The ladies' twin,' he said with a beam, as though he had personally built and furnished it himself. The bellboy placed their cases in the room, slipping silently away but not before Liberty noticed Carter quietly press a note into the lad's hand, for which he nodded and grinned his thanks. It was a superb room, both beds looking like small doubles to Liberty, and the *en suite* bathroom being a vision of black and silver marble and chrome.

'A complimentary bowl of fruit, chocolates and bottle of champagne.' The manager gestured to a massive arrangement of lilies which were perfuming the room. 'And flowers, of course.'

Carter must be spending a small fortune here this weekend for this sort of treatment, Liberty thought wryly.

'And now, if sir is ready I'll show you your room.'

'See you in reception in fifteen minutes.' Carter spoke to them both but reached out a hand and touched the side of Liberty's face as he did so.

When the door shut behind the two men, the women just had time to unpack, change and freshen up their make-up and hair before going downstairs. Liberty had chosen to wear the more understated of the two evening dresses she had brought with her, saving the one she had spent an arm and a leg on the previous week with the party in mind for the next day. Nevertheless, she knew the gunmetal-grey gown with its spaghetti straps and ruched bodice suited her colouring and, moreover, she felt comfortable in it, which was important considering she was tied up in knots at the thought of meeting Carter's parents.

She needn't have worried. From the first moment she knew she was going to get on fine with them. Like Carter, Paul Blake was tall, rugged and autocratic-looking, his thatch of thick, springy hair white and well-groomed. Mary, his wife, was surprisingly tiny but still quite beautiful in a quiet way, although the years of struggle and toil before Carter had lifted the pair of them out of the rat race showed in the lines radiating from her eyes and mouth.

'So you are Liberty Fox?' Paul Blake said softly as Carter introduced them in the cocktail lounge where his parents had been sitting waiting. 'I can see now what captivated Carter.'

'Don't, Paul, you're embarrassing her,' Mary chided at his side, ignoring the uncertain hand Liberty had proffered and reaching up on her toes to drop a birdlike kiss on Liberty's cheek. 'You look very lovely, my dear, and I'm so pleased you could come for the party tomorrow, although meeting the tribe in one fell swoop might be a little daunting.'

Liberty had been about to politely lie and say she was looking forward to it. Instead she found herself confiding, 'I'm terrified, to be truthful.'

'Don't be, we'll all be there to look after you, and if Uncle Harry comes anywhere near, Paul or Carter will block him off. We'll have them on sentry duty for the night.'

'Uncle Harry?' The others were all laughing as Liberty enquired of Carter. 'Who is Uncle Harry?'

'He's eighty if he's a day but still fancies himself as a ladies' man,' Carter said smilingly.

'He's been married six times and his present wife is a mere slip of a thing at forty,' Jennifer supplied. '*And* he gave her a baby a few months ago.' She wrinkled her nose at the thought.

'Really?' Liberty's eyes were open wide. 'And he's eighty?'

'But whether the child is Harry's as she claims is another question,' Carter said dryly. 'But he likes to believe so.'

'Carter!' His mother sounded shocked. 'Of course Catherine is Harry's; she's the image of him for one thing.'

'Mother, Catherine is small and round and bald—or nearly bald,' he corrected as his mother's mouth opened in protest. 'Of course she looks like him at the moment; that's Harry to a T. He's in his second childhood, as we all know.'

'You're a dreadful man.' But Mary was laughing as much as the others. 'Poor Harry.'

There was such an easygoing warmth between all of them. Liberty felt like a child gazing through a window into a shop packed with the best presents on earth but which she had no chance of entering. She had noticed this before with Carter and Jennifer, but now his parents were here the family unity was emphasised tenfold. They were all so very lucky, she thought wistfully.

'Ah, here's Adam.'

Carter's voice had been magnificently matter-of-fact, but as Jennifer's head shot round to the doorway where Adam was standing Liberty saw Carter's eyes were on his sister's face.

'Adam?' Jennifer said agitatedly as the tall, good-looking man in a dinner jacket began to make his way over to them. 'You didn't tell me he was coming tonight.'

'Didn't I?' Carter's voice was nonchalant. 'I must have forgotten. He mentioned he'd got plans to stay over to-morrow night so I phoned him this morning and invited him to join us. That's all right, isn't it?' He turned and spoke in an aside to his mother at this juncture. 'If he joins us tonight too?'

'Of course.' Mary was clearly delighted. 'Adam's like one of the family. He and his sister spent more time in our home than they ever did in their own when they were little,' she added to Liberty just before Adam reached them. 'Poor girl.'

With Adam's presence, the rest of the evening went far better for Liberty than she had expected. It probably wasn't very nice, she thought guiltily as the excellent five-course dinner drew to a close, but as Carter's parents were clearly just as aware of the situation between Adam and Jennifer as Carter had been, and were trying to ignore their daughter's discomfiture and embarrassment by making non-stop conversation—ably abetted by Carter who was at his most entertaining—the heat was taken off her, for which she was thankful.

There was a dance floor round which the tables were grouped, and when music started up as the waiter brought their coffee and the brandy Carter had ordered, he stood with one fluid movement and pulled her to her feet.

'Come on. I could do with working a little of that dinner off,' he said in a tone which brooked no refusal.

She couldn't argue but as she allowed herself to be led away she muttered quietly, 'I'm too full to dance.'

'Nonsense.' As he took her into his arms when they were out on the dance floor he looked down at her with hooded eyes. His next words caused her to miss a step and tread on his toes. 'Are you afraid of me?' he asked softly.

'Don't be ridiculous.' She stared at him, aware she was flushing but unable to do anything about it. 'Of course not.'

'Is it ridiculous?' he asked very seriously.

'Yes, it is.' And it was, in a way. It wasn't so much Carter she was afraid of as herself and her feelings for this strange, complex individual.

'Then why do you look at me with the eyes of a startled doe and tremble when I touch you?' he murmured in her ear.

'I don't,' she said flatly, but a tiny tremor in her voice betrayed her. She could hear it herself so he must have.

'We've grown very close over the last weeks and you know it, don't you?' His eyes had caught hers, forcing her to look at him. 'Is that why you are backing off?'

So he had known. She resorted to attack being the best defence. 'If all this is a lead up to my spending the night in your room, you can forget it,' she said scathingly.

'There's nothing I would like better than to have you in my bed.' Now he pulled her close against him, moulding her body into his so it fitted in all the right places.

'Don't, people are watching,' she whispered tensely.

He ignored this as though she hadn't spoken, continuing, 'But I would no more take you this weekend than fly to the moon. You aren't ready for me, and until you are I don't want your body. When we make love it will be just that, making love. Do you understand me, Liberty? Heart, soul, mind and body.'

It was a statement of intent and she couldn't pretend she didn't know what he was saying.

Her body seemed to be on fire and his was betraying what their closeness was doing to him. He had one arm round her waist but the other had moved to play with the silk of her hair at the nape of her neck and now she shivered, the caress of his fingers making her want his mouth on hers.

'I've no intention of letting you back off, Liberty. None.' There was a thread of steel in his voice now, his mouth close to her ear as he murmured, 'I won't allow you to put us both through hell because you are afraid of committing yourself to me. The way your mother has lived her life is nothing to do with us and you have to see that.'

The mention of her mother caused Liberty to stiffen.

'You know nothing about it,' she managed shakily. 'Nothing.'

'Because you damn well won't discuss it.' He whirled her round and out through a side door, whereupon she found herself in a small ante-room which was possibly used for drinks before a wedding reception in the main restaurant. He stood with her enclosed in his arms as he said, 'I care about you. You must see that? Damn it, everyone else can,' he added dryly.

'You said you weren't looking for anything heavy,' she reminded him desperately. 'You *said* that.'

'And I meant it at the time.'

'So what's changed?'

'Me. I admit it.' His hold on her didn't loosen despite her attempt to prise his hands away from her waist. 'But I also said I like honesty and truth in a relationship, remember? And that holds. So…' he smiled down at her with glittering eyes '…I thought I'd better be straight with you. I want you, Liberty, but not for a week or a month or whatever. You're not that kind of girl.'

She didn't know what to say so she said the first thing that came into her head through her whirling thoughts. 'What kind of girl am I, then?' And immediately wished she hadn't.

'The kind that makes a guy think that maybe for ever isn't so implausible after all.'

She became very still in his arms. 'This isn't fair, Carter.' Her voice was barely a whisper. 'I told you at the beginning where I stood.'

'It was different then.' And it had been, damn it. They hadn't known each other then. Over the last weeks they had packed more talking, more laughter, more of what made a couple a couple than some folk shared in a decade. He knew it. And she knew it. And that was why she was scared to death. This wasn't one-sided. She wanted him as much as he wanted her. No, he wouldn't compromise at want. *Loved* him as much as he loved her. They wouldn't be having this conversation if she didn't.

'I haven't led you on,' she said dully.

'I'm not saying you have,' he said quietly.

'I… I can't be the sort of person you want me to be.'

'Tell me you don't love me,' he challenged directly, studying her with narrowed eyes. 'Say it and mean it and I'll forget all this right now. But I shall know if you're lying.'

Her heart was pounding and there was a lump in her throat which caused a physical ache. How could she tell him that?

'I know your mother left you and your father but *he* stayed, didn't he? Look at him, not her.'

He didn't understand, but how could he? She didn't understand the way she felt herself. Logic didn't come into it.

'You haven't said it.' His voice was very soft.

'What?' She played for time, her head whirling.

'That you don't love me.' Her body was rigid; he could feel her like a piece of board in his arms, but they had to talk, damn it. He was inhaling the perfume that came from her skin and hair, drinking it in, and it seemed impossible that she could ever walk away from him. It *was* impossible. It had to be.

'It's not a question of love.' She swallowed, her head falling. 'My mother thought she loved my father in the early days; she's told me that. And then she fell in love with someone else and then someone else…'

'You are not your mother.' Suddenly he wanted to shake her.

But she had her mother's blood flowing through her

veins as well as her father's. The deeply buried dread which had been in her subconscious since she had reached the age of understanding forced its way into the light. She took a shuddering breath but she couldn't speak.

'Do you hear me, Liberty? You are not like her.'

'How do you know?' She raised her eyes to his, willing herself not to break down and cry. 'How on earth do you know?'

'Because I know you.'

'Carter, five weeks ago you weren't aware I existed, so how can you know me?'

He stared at her, his eyes very steady, very calm. 'Because what we have doesn't rely on time,' he said evenly. 'You're my other half. I feel it in my bones, my blood, my head, my heart. I knew you the minute I met you, although I didn't let myself believe it then. I told myself this would be another fling—nothing serious, but exciting for as long as it lasted. I was kidding myself. I've had women since I was seventeen years old and still wet behind the ears. I'm not wet behind the ears any more and I recognise the real thing when I see it.'

The real thing? Was he talking marriage here? The panic she felt showed in her face and after a long moment he sighed. 'What am I going to do with you?' he said very quietly and he was not smiling. 'Look, you acknowledge there's something between us, yes? Something good? Something very good?'

She nodded. It would be useless to deny it.

'Something you haven't felt for anyone else?'

She nodded again and he felt a surge of elation which he checked before it took over. 'And it's scared you to death,' he continued flatly. 'So much so you wanted out.'

She looked away, her heart beating frantically like a hard little tennis ball against her ribcage.

'Well, now it's out in the open—how you feel and how I feel, and we both know where we stand. In spite of that, or maybe because of it, I see no reason for our relationship not to continue the way it's been going. Let's relax and play it by ear, okay? The time thing bothers you. I can understand that. I can't pretend to get in your head, but I can accept this has happened like a bolt from the blue. I feel the same.'

'You do?'

'Yeah. Amazingly, you're not the only one who is allowed to feel the axis of their world has suddenly shifted,' he said wryly. 'So, we continue seeing each other?' Before she could answer, he took her face between his hands and kissed her. It was a long, sweet, aching kiss, a kiss which seemed to confirm everything he had told her, which said he loved her.

When it was over she was trembling, but she forced herself to say, 'What if the time thing doesn't work to your advantage like you think it will? What if things go wrong the more we know about each other? I... I don't want to hurt you.'

Hurt him? It'd kill him. Carter grinned. 'I'm a big boy,' he said lazily, forcing his body to relax along with his voice. 'Don't worry about it.'

His reward was when she lifted her hand and touched the side of his face in a soft cupping action that carried a wealth of emotion in its tenderness.

'We'd better get back to the others.' He had taken her hand and kissed it before he spoke, and now he put an arm round her waist and led her through to the dance floor, where they were confronted with the cheering sight of Jennifer in Adam's arms as he whisked her about the dance floor.

When they got to their table they hadn't even sat down

before Mary said, 'What do you think?' as she inclined her head towards the dance floor. 'They look like they're getting on well.'

'It's a start.' Carter glanced at Liberty as he spoke and she had the feeling he wasn't talking about the two on the dance floor.

'I do hope Jennifer lets him see how she feels.' Mary glanced at Liberty, her brow wrinkled. 'They've wasted so much time already. Poor Adam hasn't known where he's stood with her.'

'It's up to them now.' Paul's voice held a mild warning note as he spoke to his wife. 'They're both adults and not young kids, and for all we know one or the other of them doesn't feel the same any more. Don't you say anything, Mary.'

'I wouldn't dream of it.' Mary tossed her head huffily, and then, as her husband reached across and squeezed her hand, she added, 'I just hope Jennifer *says* something,' and Paul groaned softly, glancing at Carter, who grinned sympathetically.

Whether it was this which caused Carter's father to say, once Jennifer and Adam returned to the table, 'Well, we'll leave you young things to it and take a cab home now, if that's all right. It's going to be a long day tomorrow and we're not spring chickens any more,' wasn't clear, but Liberty suspected so. Certainly Carter's mother's feet hardly touched the ground.

Once they had seen Paul and Mary off from reception, Jennifer declared herself ready for bed and Liberty quickly agreed. Apparently the men were sharing a twin room along the corridor from their room, so they all went up in the lift together, Jennifer and Adam disappearing into their respective quarters when Carter paused outside the girls' room.

'Tactful, aren't they?'

He grinned at her, and Liberty couldn't help smiling back even as she said, 'You *did* make it pretty obvious.'

'That I wanted to say goodnight in private? Too true.' His arms folded around her waist and tugged her into the cradle of his hips. He dipped his head, covering her lips in a hard, hungry kiss. Her arms wound round his neck, her hands sliding into the blackness of his hair, which smelt of shampoo.

The kiss was a kiss of infinite desire, the thundering of his heart testifying to his arousal as blatantly as did his maleness, the feel of his hips grinding against hers leaving her in no doubt that his need was as great as her own.

'I could eat you up, do you know that?' When he finally broke off the kiss he was breathing hard and his voice was a groan. His hands moved to the swell of her breasts, the silk of her dress causing his fingers to glide with a touch as light as down over the sensitised flesh. Her nipples hardened in response, and as his mouth again took hers she was ready when his tongue tasted the sweetness within.

The muscles across his back were tense as her hands slid across his broad frame, relishing the feel of the powerful male body. He moved her against the wall of the corridor and for a crazy moment she was tempted to hoist up the dress and wrap her hips round him. It was enough to break the madness.

'Carter… No.' She flattened the palms of her hands on his chest, pushing to emphasise her words. 'We're out here, anyone could see us.'

He stopped, but it still took a moment or two before he straightened reluctantly, shaking his head as he said, 'I can't believe what you do to me,' a touch of ruefulness in his voice. 'Get in that room quick before I forget all my good intentions and carry you off somewhere.'

She smiled, but now she was out of his arms her lack of control appalled her. What sort of message was she sending? He only had to touch her and she melted for him, but you didn't stay in bed twenty-four hours a day in a relationship, did you? she argued to herself. How did she know this wasn't just fierce sexual attraction—for him as well as for her? Something which would burn itself out, leaving ashes in its place and just a charred lingering odour.

'Stop thinking.'

She didn't know her face was revealing her thoughts, but as he halted her withdrawal into herself she gazed at him with eyes that had turned as black as ebony.

'I mean it, Liberty. You're tired, emotionally and physically. Don't go on any more witch-hunts tonight. Go and take a shower and go to sleep. You can dream of me as long as they're good dreams, okay?'

She hooked a strand of hair behind her ear and laughed nervously. 'You sound like a shrink.'

He held up protesting hands. 'It's just plain common sense, sweetheart.'

Sweetheart. He had never called her that before and she found she liked it. 'Goodnight, Carter,' she said softly.

'Goodnight.' He didn't move from where he now stood leaning against the wall, powerful arms crossed over his chest, merely continuing to watch her with brooding eyes until the door of her room closed.

# CHAPTER SEVEN

LIBERTY hadn't expected to sleep at all when she climbed into bed after a long, warm shower but, to her amazement, after she said goodnight to a sleepy Jennifer, she didn't remember anything else till morning.

She awoke to hear Jennifer was already in the shower, and when the other girl walked through to the bedroom, her hair wrapped turban fashion in a towel and a bath sheet round her body, Jennifer smiled at her ruefully. 'I needed to do something to hide the ravages of an almost sleepless night,' Carter's sister said, plumping herself down on the end of Liberty's bed. 'Do the shadows under my eyes look too bad?'

Liberty gazed into the fresh, pretty face and smiled. 'You look just great,' she assured her firmly. 'I promise.'

'I went to sleep in a twinkling and then woke up an hour later and that was that,' Jennifer said mournfully. 'Liberty, do you think it means anything, the fact that Adam's come up by himself without a girlfriend in tow?'

These two had to be the dimmest pair in history! Liberty shook her head, deciding some straight talking was in order. 'Jen, he's crazy about you; a blind man could see that,' she said exasperatedly. 'Why do you think he's never stayed with a girl for more than two minutes? But after all that's happened you need to give him a bit of encouragement; surely you see that? It wasn't him who started messing about with other people and then got married, after all.'

'But what if I say something, do something, and then

he doesn't want to know?' Jennifer said weakly. 'What then?'

'You're no worse off than you are now.' Liberty stared at her. 'And, to be honest, I think you owe it to him to make the first move.'

'You do?' It was uncertain. 'Really?'

'Yes, I do,' Liberty said firmly. 'And if you end up with egg on your face, take it on the chin.'

'The egg?' Jennifer giggled before her face straightened again and she almost wailed, 'Oh, I'm mad about him, Liberty. I'll just die if he gives me the cold shoulder.'

'You wouldn't and he won't. Now, pull out all the stops and titivate while I have my shower, and then we'll go down to breakfast. And for goodness' sake don't waste the day thinking about what you're going to do. Do something straight away so you can actually enjoy this evening.'

'You really think he likes me, don't you?'

'No, I don't think he likes you, Jen. I think he loves you.' Liberty shook her head in exasperation. 'Trust me.'

'Okay.' Jennifer straightened her shoulders, thrusting her chin up. 'I'll do it. At breakfast. Somehow I'll do it and if it goes wrong, well, I've only myself to blame for how I was when we were younger. If I don't do it I'll never know.'

'It won't go wrong.'

Once in the shower, Liberty stood for some minutes in the warm, silky flow, trying to moderate her racing heart-beat and the churning in her stomach at the thought of seeing Carter again after their conversation last night.

Why was it always so much easier to give someone else advice about their love life? she wondered ruefully. She'd sounded like an old sage talking to Jennifer and yet she was the last person on earth who should be talking about love and commitment. Talk about the pot calling the kettle black!

She dug her fingers into her scalp as she washed her hair, for all the world as though she was washing all the doubt and uncertainty away with the foaming suds.

Carter had said he'd never felt the way he felt about her in all his life, that he had changed, but how did she know that for sure? By his own admission he had never had to wait to get a woman into bed before, so it might just be that the challenge she had unwittingly presented, the thrill of the chase, was keeping sexual tension to a pitch where he imagined all sorts of things. There was an obvious solution to that, of course.

She rubbed in conditioner, frowning slightly. But if she gave herself to him and in a few weeks or months they did part company, would she ever recover from the fallout? Loving him as she did, it wouldn't just be her body she was committing, but her heart, soul and everything that made her her.

The conditioner rinsed away, she stepped out of the shower and began to dry herself with a fluffy bath sheet. But it would be one more barrier removed; that fact was inescapable. Oh, she just didn't know what to do or how to play this. She raised her head, staring at her reflection in the bathroom mirror. There was no answer in the eyes of the tragic-faced woman looking back at her. But then she hadn't expected one.

Play it by ear. Carter's words of the night before came back to her, and she nodded to them. It was the only answer in this tangle she'd managed to get herself into. She couldn't imagine life without him now, but she couldn't imagine a for ever scenario either. Hell, she was a mess. Why he was bothering with her at all she didn't know. There must be any number of young, uncomplicated, eager things out there just champing at the bit to get into his bed.

Once back in the bedroom she dressed swiftly in smart casual trousers and a white cashmere waist-length jumper, but in spite of taking time to dry her hair carefully and apply a light coating of foundation and mascara, she still had to wait another ten minutes until Jennifer was satisfied that her own make-up and hair was just right.

The other woman's jitteriness was infectious, and as they travelled down in the lift Liberty found herself wringing her hands before she caught sight of herself in the mirrored panels. She forced herself to relax, taking a long, deep, calming breath. What with Jennifer and Adam, and her own feelings about Carter, she would be a nervous wreck at the end of this weekend if she didn't pull herself together.

The two men were already sitting in the restaurant and Carter lifted a beckoning hand as they walked in. They both had a glass of orange juice in front of them but had obviously waited before ordering. Carter looked so delicious it was with great forbearance that Liberty didn't fling herself into his lap.

'Good morning.' They had both risen at the women's approach and as Adam smiled at Jennifer, Carter bent and placed the lightest of kisses on Liberty's mouth. Which really shouldn't have ignited the fire in the pit of her stomach, she reflected helplessly as she took her seat.

'Sleep well?'

Adam's enquiry of Jennifer was clearly a social pleasantry but her reply was anything but. 'No,' Carter's sister said, very quietly but very distinctly. 'I lay awake all night wondering if I had the nerve to admit to you what a complete fool I've been in the past and ask for another chance.'

You could have heard a pin drop. Liberty froze, her eyes

on the cutlery in front of her. Carter's hand, which had been reaching for his orange juice, hesitated briefly before manfully carrying on but once it reached its target it just remained there. The whole world was waiting with bated breath.

Adam must have been staring at Jennifer dumbstruck because her voice was tiny when she said, 'Can you ever forgive me? I know you'll have to think about it but—'

'I've thought.' Adam's voice was husky and low, and now Liberty did raise her head to look at him. What she saw in his face made her swallow hard. 'Let's get out of here. Carter, you don't mind…?'

'Go ahead.' Carter was grinning like the Cheshire cat.

Jennifer was now pink and trembling and as Adam took her hand and fairly galloped her out of the restaurant Carter said in true brotherly fashion, 'Thank heavens for that; she's been driving me as nuts as she has him. I hope he doesn't make it too easy for her.'

'You don't mean that.' Liberty smiled at him, the suddenness of Jennifer's bravery both amazing her and filling her with admiration. 'And you know he will. He loves her.'

'There is that.' He smiled at her, his voice taking on a dry tone as he said, 'I hope you're taking note. You know we might have got it wrong with the two per cent we talked about a few weeks ago. Perhaps more couples make it than we gave credit for. It's a thought, isn't it?'

She might have known he wouldn't miss any opportunity to press his case, but looking at him all she could think of was how much she loved him and how incredibly lucky Jennifer and Adam were. They might have had their own share of misery and heartache but they would make it now, she was sure of it. But as for her and Carter…

'Anyway, I hate to bring things down to a more basic level but my stomach is beginning to think my throat has been cut. If you are ready we'll order before we help our-selves to cereal and so on. I've a feeling we might not see much of Jennifer and Adam before tonight.'

Probably due to the sea air, Liberty found she thor-oughly enjoyed her breakfast. Carter demolished twice as much as she did, along with several rounds of toast and preserves and a pot of coffee. She gazed at him in awe.

'Do you always eat such a hearty breakfast?' she asked him as he sat back in his seat, replete at last.

'I'm a big boy,' he said mildly. 'Or hadn't you noticed?'

She ignored the glint in his eyes. 'Do you need to be overseeing the preparations for the party tonight or what-ever?' she asked as they rose from their seats. 'I can easily occupy myself, so don't worry about me.'

'Not this morning.' He took her hand in his. 'Probably not this afternoon either but I just wanted to be around in case of last-minute hitches. I want this to be perfect for my parents. When they married there was no money for a reception or anything of that nature. This is to make up for that.'

She stared at him. When she had first met him he had portrayed the image of hard-headed businessman who was as ruthless in his private life as he was in his work. And that was part of him, she knew that. But he had allowed her to glimpse the inner man now and again, and this had happened more of late. And the inner man was... disturbing. Wonderfully so.

'Fancy a walk along the sea front?' he asked as they made their way to the lift. 'I like the smell of the sea.'

She nodded. The day was cold but bright and sunny, and with the English weather in mind she had brought warm clothes, along with sheepskin boots and a cosy hat which enclosed her ears, for just such an eventuality.

She exited her room, muffled like an Eskimo, just as

Carter came along the corridor from his quarters dressed in a black leather jacket and black denim jeans. He looked so sexy she found it difficult to breathe for a moment.

'I thought it might be cold,' she said breathlessly in an effort to explain her mummified appearance.

'It will be,' he assured her, dropping a quick kiss on her nose. 'I might come under that hat with you.'

The tiered gardens of the hotel led down to the sea front and the nearer they got to the sea the more bitter the wind became. Once the sea was in front of them the winter sun was a pale flash of light on the icy water, but beautiful nevertheless.

She had to grasp each moment of this weekend, Liberty told herself, without questioning why it was so important. She had to take each experience deep into her psyche, and the crashing white-tipped waves and harsh calls of the seagulls in the blue sky above were part of the haunting beauty.

'Warm enough?' Carter asked as they began to walk towards the beach. He was holding her securely against him, which was a mixed blessing. She appreciated the warmth his big masculine body provided, but the feel of the hard angles and planes and the tantalising thrill of being enclosed and protected made her a little light-headed.

'I'm fine,' she assured him weakly, the fact that the sea wind took her words and whipped them away providing a welcome cover for her body's betrayal.

She knew her nose would be as red as a beetroot by the time they had elevenses in a little café along the sea front, and it was immensely irritating that Carter seemed oblivious to the cold. She said as much once they were ensconced at a table by the window drinking hot chocolate. 'It's a male thing,' he assured her solemnly, his eyes dancing. 'Weak, fragile woman and big strong man, you know.'

She said a rude word and he laughed out loud. Ridiculously, the warmth and ease of the exchange hit her like a blow between the ribs, the ever present danger his attraction held re-emphasised.

Carter noticed the way her eyes dropped from his to the mug held between her fingers and guessed the reason for it. She looked like a little child in that hat and with her nose pink-tipped, he thought, a stab of pain making itself felt. But Liberty was no child. She was a woman, a beautiful and desirable woman who was determined to keep him somewhere on the perimeter of her life. No, not exactly the perimeter, he corrected in the next moment, but nowhere near where he wanted to be.

He took a pull at the hot chocolate. So it was up to him to scale the battlements, and he would. If it took his last breath he would. The somewhat lofty ideal mocked him, causing his mouth to twist in self-deprecation as the more carnal side of him admitted the need for her was achingly intense. But he could and would control that.

He stretched out his hand, lifting her chin so her eyes met his. 'You're thinking again,' he said softly. 'Let yourself feel instead. Go beyond that formidable solicitor's mind which has everything slotted and labelled into neat files.'

She forced a smile but it was an effort. 'If I was thinking at all it was just how nice it is to be in the warm, drinking chocolate and looking out into the wind and cold,' she lied lightly.

One dark eyebrow quirked.

Ignore it, she told herself quickly as a desire to defend herself rose hot and strong. He wanted to provoke a re-action, to keep probing the wound, and she wasn't about to go down that path. 'I wonder how Jennifer and Adam are getting on,' she said flatly.

'Oh, so do I.' It was lazily sarcastic but she pretended she didn't notice.

'It would make the evening for your parents if they saw the two of them had got together, wouldn't it?' she said determinedly. 'The icing on the cake, so to speak.'

He nodded, his eyes silver-grey in the light streaming in through the window. 'My mother is longing to be a grandmother.' He took her hand in his, turning it over and stroking the palm with his other hand. 'She'd just about given up on the pair of us.' His eyes were unblinking as they looked into hers, his firm, sculptured mouth curving cynically even though his voice was bland and conversational.

Liberty tried very hard not to think of Carter and babies, of making babies— She cleared her throat, extracting her hand from his as she said, 'I'll just pop to the Ladies' before we go back.' And she fled to its dubious sanctuary.

Once in the tiny washroom which held one toilet, one washbasin and a cracked mirror and smelt strongly of bleach, she stared at herself in the spotted glass. Her nose was as red as she'd feared, she noticed wryly. She turned away, leaning against the wall as she asked herself what it was Carter saw in her. She just didn't get it.

The arrival of a big fat matron with a squawking baby cut short the introspection, and after Liberty had edged round the woman she made her way back to Carter, who was sitting looking moodily out of the window in the moment before he saw her.

After lunch, during which Jennifer and Adam were conspicuous by their absence, Liberty pleaded a headache and escaped to her room after telling Carter she would join him a little later.

It was cowardly, she admitted to herself as she flung

herself down on the bed after closing the curtains, but she really did have an ache behind her eyes caused mainly by the ache in her heart probably. It shouldn't be like this, should it? Romance, love, call it what you would. Wasn't it supposed to be all thrills and excitement and never wanting the feeling to end?

She tossed and turned a little before padding through to the bathroom and getting a glass of water, whereupon she took two of the aspirin she kept in her handbag for emergencies. The headache was fast becoming a major throb, and she slipped off her trousers and jumper, snuggling down under the covers in her bra and panties. She'd lie quietly for half an hour or so until it subsided, she thought, and then she would go and find Carter to see if she could help with anything.

She awoke three hours later to a knock at the door and found the room in shadowed twilight. She glanced at her watch and then couldn't believe her eyes. She'd slept the afternoon away. She couldn't remember doing that since she was a child. As the knock sounded again she flung back the duvet and reached for her silk robe, which she'd slung on to a chair at the side of the bed that morning. Pulling the belt tight, she padded to the door and opened it.

'How's the head?' Carter was leaning against the doorpost, his posture lazy but his grey eyes tight on her face.

'Carter, I'm so sorry,' she said quickly. 'I only intended to lie down for a few minutes after I'd taken some aspirin but I must have fallen asleep. I was going to help you with things.'

'No need.' His somewhat severe expression had mellowed at the obvious sincerity and he stroked back a lock of her hair with one finger. 'Look, Adam and Jen are in my room and they've some news for us. Have you got your key?'

'Shouldn't I put some clothes on?' she asked, flustered.

'Not on my account.' He grinned at her. 'Anyway, you look perfectly decent in this silky thing; it covers more of you than normal.' It also clung in all the right places and he didn't think she was wearing much beneath it. His loins tightened and his voice was slightly husky when he said, 'Just get the key and come along. They're waiting.'

Carter and Adam's room was identical to the women's, but as Liberty entered it she wasn't taking note of the décor. Adam was standing with one arm round Jennifer's shoulders and from the beam on both their faces Liberty assumed the news was good.

'Liberty!' Jennifer reached out her hands, her voice rushed and excited. 'We wanted you and Carter to be the first to know. Look.' She stretched out her left hand, twirling it around so that the solitaire diamond engagement ring flashed in the artificial light. 'We're engaged!'

'Oh, Jen!' Liberty hugged the other woman as Carter stepped forward and shook Adam's hand. 'Jen, I'm so pleased.'

'I would say you're a quick worker,' Carter said to his friend, 'but considering this has taken over a decade to come about, I won't.'

'We want to get married in the spring,' Jennifer went on, 'just a quiet wedding with a few friends and family, but in a church. I wouldn't feel married if we didn't do it in a church. Will you and Carter be our witnesses?'

'And it goes without saying I want you as my best man,' Adam added when he could get a word in edgeways, clapping Carter on the back, a grin on his face which stretched from ear to ear. 'If you will, of course.'

'And you as my bridesmaid,' Jennifer chimed in again

to Liberty. 'I shall only have you. I did the five bridesmaids and a page boy last time and I want this to be completely different.'

'It will be,' Adam assured her dryly. 'Not least because
this is for ever.'

'I know.' Jennifer turned from Liberty and leapt into his
arms, her legs wrapped round his hips as they kissed.

A polite knock at the door interrupted the delirium. As
Adam put Jennifer down he said, 'That'll be the champagne. I thought we'd toast the future together, just the
four of us.'

Liberty kept the smile on her face with some effort as
the waiter brought in the champagne in an ice bucket,
along with a bowl of strawberries and a plate of canapés—
compliments of the management, the waiter informed them
smilingly. She was thrilled for Jennifer and Adam, over
the moon, but all this talk of bridesmaids and witnesses…
She didn't know if she and Carter would still be together
next week, let alone in the spring. But she couldn't very
well say so right now. She would just have to go along
with everything for the moment and sort it out with
Jennifer later, once the initial hubbub had died down.

They drank the champagne and ate the strawberries and
canapés amid much laughter; Carter and Adam in fine form
as they ribbed and chaffed each other in the way only very
good friends could, and Liberty felt herself relaxing a little.

At five o'clock Jennifer declared she needed bags of
time to get ready for the party, pulling Liberty to the door
and giggling like a schoolgirl. She was on such a high that
Liberty wondered if she'd ever come down. As they
stepped into the corridor Adam caught hold of Liberty's
arm, his voice soft as he said, 'Jen told me what you said
to her this morning. Thanks, Liberty. I owe you.' And he
kissed her lightly on the cheek.

'Have I missed something vital here?'

Carter raised dark eyebrows and Adam grinned at him. 'Seems so, all knowing one.'

'I just said to Jen that she needed to make it plain how she felt,' Liberty said embarrassedly, knowing in advance how Carter would take it. 'That's all. Nothing much.'

He was, however, quite restrained, contenting himself with a glance of cool amusement as he murmured, 'Out of the mouths of babes…'

Once back in their room, the two women began to get ready in something of a spin. Jennifer's animation and feverish happiness was infectious, and Liberty found she was enjoying herself as they giggled at nothing with nervous excitement. She put Jennifer's hair up for her, persuading the thick waves into an elegant chignon which made the most of Carter's sister's elfin features and big eyes, especially when teamed with the red and gold asymmetric evening dress Jennifer was wearing.

'Do you think Adam and I ought to have a quiet word with Mum and Dad before you and Carter come down?' Jennifer asked suddenly. It had been arranged that the four of them would meet Paul and Mary Blake for cocktails half an hour before the guests were due to start arriving.

Liberty nodded; she'd been thinking the same thing herself. 'I think I'd like that if I was them,' she said quietly.

'It will give Adam a chance to ask for my hand,' Jennifer said with a smile, her eyes as bright as if she'd had a magnum of champagne instead of just one glass. 'He said he wants to do that, you know, ask formally.'

'Does he?' Adam went up another notch in Liberty's eyes. 'Well, I definitely think it would be best, then. He doesn't want Carter and me breathing down his neck when he's doing the in-law bit.'

'It's ten past seven. Mum and Dad'll be here before half

past, if I know them. I'll go and get Adam now and tell him what we've decided. Shall I tell Carter to knock on the door when he's ready to go down?'

Liberty nodded. She had finished her own hair and make-up; all she needed to do now was to slip into her dress and apply a touch of gloss to her lipstick.

Once Jennifer had left the room in a swirl of red and gold, Liberty slipped off her robe and went across to the dress she had hanging on the outside of the wardrobe door. Jennifer had oohed and aahed over the exquisitely elegant sheer sequinned and beaded tulle gown, and it was fabulous, there was no doubt about it. She had bought some dangling rock crystal earrings to set off the criss-cross gilet-style of the bodice which could still be seen even with her hair loose, but as she gazed at the beautiful dress she had a moment of misgiving.

It clung to her like a second skin and, although her flesh-coloured bra and panties made the dress more than decent, it was definitely the sexiest thing she had ever worn. But she had wanted to look good for Carter. She had wanted his eyes to be on her and no one else. She wrinkled her nose at herself, her brows coming together in a perplexed frown as she tried to rationalise the tumult of emotions which had been swirling about inside her since the day they had met.

But she couldn't. If she was being truthful, she just couldn't. She wanted him to want her like he'd never wanted another woman in his life but, contrarily, it also scared her to death.

But she hadn't felt like this with Gerard, not for a second. *Because she hadn't loved Gerard.* He hadn't even begun to touch the inner core of her, so that had made his apparent devotion and love quite safe.

Oh stop it, she told herself irritably. Get dressed and stop thinking, as Carter would say. Oh, Carter…

She forced herself to take the dress off the hanger and let it slip over her head. It fell in glorious smoothness to her feet, and suddenly she felt she very much needed another glass of champagne! It had looked like a million dollars in the very exclusive shop she had entered with fear and trepidation, but now, fully made up and with her hair down, it was… She couldn't find a word to adequately describe what it did for her, but she wished she could bottle it and bring it out on a day when she was feeling fat and spotty.

When she heard Carter's knock at the door she had been sitting on the edge of the bed for some minutes, willing herself to calm down as she attempted to flick through a magazine.

Her sandals were so high they demanded a completely different way of walking, but in the two weeks since she'd acquired them she had been in training. Now she swayed over to the door with consummate ease, opening it and then experiencing a thunderbolt of a shock herself.

She had known Carter was going to dress up, but the black dinner jacket and tie were new—at least she hadn't seen them before—and even the white tux he'd worn on occasion couldn't compete with the style and fit of what he was wearing tonight. His dark hair was slicked back, his tanned face carried a delicious scent of aftershave on clean male skin as he bent forward and kissed her—he was every woman's fantasy of what she would like to find in her stocking on Christmas Day.

'You look sensational,' he said softly, the husky quality to his voice telling her he meant every word. 'Every eye is going to be on you tonight.'

'I hope not.' She looked faintly alarmed. 'It's your parents' evening, and Jennifer and Adam's, of course.'

'Here.' He handed her a long, slim box from his pocket. 'I was going to get you a corsage and then I thought you might be wearing a dress which didn't lend itself to it, so I played safe. I thought this would go with anything.'

'What is it?' She looked at the box as if it was going to bite her. 'You shouldn't have bought me anything.'

'Open it and see,' he suggested with the cool laziness he always adopted when he was faintly unsure of himself. She blinked, wondering where that thought had come from, but then she realised it was true. It was a self-protection he adopted.

She didn't like the flood of tenderness the knowledge evoked, and it made her stiffen even before she opened the box and saw the sparkling diamond bracelet it held. 'Carter…' She raised huge eyes to his dark face. 'Why? I mean it's not even my birthday.'

'Do you like it?' he asked softly.

'It's beautiful.' It was, exquisitely so, but it must also have been wildly expensive. She stared at it helplessly.

'Then that's why,' he said quietly. 'I wanted to give you a present, that's all.'

For a second she had the weirdest feeling that a trap was opening up in front of her, a trap with glutinous jaws that having once seized her would never let her go. Her voice shaking, she said, 'It's beautiful, but I can't possibly accept it. It's…it's far too much.'

'Of course it isn't.' His tone was quiet but there was steel under it as he sensed she was being more than just polite.

'Carter—' she raised panicky eyes to his '—I wouldn't feel right taking such an expensive gift.'

He stared at her for a moment before shaking his head

in a way which fully spoke of his bewilderment. 'You are probably the only woman I have ever met who would say that and mean it,' he said flatly. 'With any of the others it would have been a way of playing coy.'

The others. And there had been others, lots of others; he hadn't tried to fool her about that. Why she suddenly felt such a burning jealousy she didn't know, but it made her voice sharp. 'It's too much,' she repeated, her cheeks burning but her eyes resolute. 'I know you meant well but I can't take it.'

'It's nothing.' His voice was dispassionate now, remote. 'A trinket. Put it on and let's forget about it.'

Her mother had always inveigled presents out of her lovers. A memory she didn't even know she had surfaced, that of her father holding aloft a gold watch, still in its box, and shouting at her mother, asking where she had got it from. And her mother, eyes flashing and mouth taut, snarling that it was none of his business, that if he wouldn't buy her nice things there were others who would. She didn't remember her mother being around after that, so she guessed that must have been about the time she had walked out on them both.

'It's not a trinket.' She was very pale now in sharp contrast to a moment before. 'It's a beautiful bracelet and I don't want you to think I'm not grateful—'

'But?' His voice was calm, too calm.

'But I can't accept it.' Her voice was resolute.

He swore, and his muttered oath had all the power of a shout. 'What's so wrong about my giving you a gift?' he asked after a moment or two when she saw him take visible control of himself. 'For crying out loud, Liberty, what?'

Nothing and everything. She couldn't explain to him because she didn't understand herself.

Carter checked the urge to step forward and shake her until she saw sense, and instead steadied his voice to a hard, cold flatness. He held out his hand and when she returned the box to him he slipped it in his jacket pocket, saying, 'It's forgotten, okay? It never happened. Now, shall we go and join the others?' he suggested icily, turning from her.

This was awful, terrible. She had ruined the party for him and he had been so pleased he was giving his parents the wedding reception they'd never had. And Jennifer and Adam; it would take the edge off everything. She didn't know what to say or do to make things better. 'Carter, I'm sorry.'

He shrugged. 'Like I said, forget it. I have. Now, if you are ready we'd better go down. They'll be waiting.'

When she didn't answer or move he turned back with an abrupt movement which spoke of irritation. Then, as he noticed the gleam of tears he became still, and this time when he swore it was soft and desperate but his arms had reached out to enfold her into him. They stood quite still for what seemed like an eternity. She could feel his heart thudding and the smell and bigness of his muscled body enveloped all her senses to the point where she would have given the world to remain for ever in his embrace.

'It's not you, or…or the bracelet.' Her voice came muffled from against his chest. 'I can't explain.'

'I'm not asking for explanations.'

She raised her head, her eyes locking with his. 'Yes, you are,' she said softly, 'and you have every right to. It's a wonderful gift. Anyone would be thrilled to receive it.'

He stared at her, aware they were at a crossroads and not knowing what to do or say to get guidance for the right road. The logical male side of him wanted to sit her down and force her to confront her gremlins so they could be done with all the messing around, but something inside told him he couldn't rush her. Nevertheless, he felt something of a shock tactic was owed him. 'How do you see your mother, Liberty?' he asked quietly, seeing the recoil in her eyes but tilting her chin to meet his eyes when she would have looked away. 'As a person, as a human being, I mean. Because this is all linked with her, isn't it? This is another piece of the jigsaw.'

He thought she would refuse to answer but after a moment she nodded, her eyes misted with tears.

'So, how do you see her? Forget she's your mother for a minute and tell me what you see.'

'A black widow spider.'

It was so soft he could barely hear the whisper but it said more than talking half the night would have done. Carter found he needed to think about this one. 'Do you need to do anything to your make-up before we go down?' he asked tactfully, without mentioning the smudges under her eyes.

Liberty nodded and sniffed. 'I won't be a minute.'

She was five but he wasn't counting.

# CHAPTER EIGHT

THE evening went like clockwork, but then Carter had paid a great deal of money to make sure it did. Liberty stood enclosed within Carter's arm with his parents and Jennifer and Adam to welcome the guests as they arrived, and it was clear to everyone that her daughter's engagement *was* the icing on the cake as far as Carter's mother was concerned.

They were such a close-knit family, Liberty thought, and there was no doubt that Mary Blake was the axis around which the others revolved. Her husband was clearly as much in love with her as he'd ever been, and Carter and Jennifer adored her too. Which was right and proper, she knew that, but she just found it all a little too good to be true. Which was horrible, she acknowledged silently, because she didn't think they were putting on an act, far from it. This was family as it should be.

After everyone had arrived, the six of them took their places at the top table and both Carter and Jennifer gave a speech in honour of their parents. Both children's words were moving and Liberty found she was blinking back tears through it all, the feeling of being outside with her nose pressed up against the window-pane stronger than ever. Which was her fault, totally her fault, she reasoned, because she only had to say the word and she could be in this wonderful family.

But for how long? a little voice deep inside whispered in her ear. You don't think it would last, do you? You don't think a man like Carter wouldn't realise in time he'd made a mistake? How long would it take him to conclude you are nothing special, just an ordinary woman who can never be what he really wants you to be? A woman who would let him down…

After the speeches the five-course meal was enjoyed with relish, the buzz of conversation and sound of laughter from all the tables dotted around the vast room confirming everyone was having a great time.

Mary and Paul took the floor for the first dance amid much cheering and whooping by those present, and as the champagne continued to flow everyone let their hair down with gusto. The dance floor was constantly buzzing.

Liberty had been introduced to everyone by Carter as they had stood in the line-up at the beginning of the evening; now he made sure they had plenty of dances together without interruption. He danced wonderfully. She felt she was floating in his arms half the time and, as always when she let her senses rule her mind, she felt she'd died and gone to heaven as he held her close. She felt she didn't want the evening to end.

It was close to midnight and they were just returning to the table preparatory to sampling the magnificent hot buffet which had been brought in to be served on the stroke of twelve, when Adam appeared at their side. 'Jennifer's exhausted,' he whispered, gesturing to the far edge of the room where Carter's sister was sitting in one of the comfy sofas apparently fast asleep. 'I'm taking her up to her room.'

Carter and Liberty followed him across to where Jennifer sat, Carter's face wry as he looked down at his sibling. 'Jen is also a little the worse for wear,' he murmured dryly, and then, glancing at Adam's flushed face, he added, 'Do you want Liberty and I to help you with her?'

'I can look after her,' Adam said, yawning widely.

'Who's going to be looking after you while you're looking after her?' Carter enquired caustically.

'Very funny.' Adam yawned again, and then, as Jennifer opened bleary eyes, said, 'Come on, Jen, let's go up.'

'I've said goodnight to Mum and Dad,' Jennifer said to Carter as Adam helped her to her feet. 'I'm just dead beat what with not sleeping last night and then all the excitement today. I can't keep my eyes open now.'

'I don't suppose the copious champagne helped much either,' Carter said with brotherly frankness.

Jennifer giggled tiredly. 'Not much,' she agreed, 'but it was nice. Wonderful, in fact. The best night of my life.'

Carter smiled back, his voice soft as he bent and placed a kiss on her cheek. 'Sleep well, infant.'

'Thank you, big bruv.' Jennifer stood on tiptoe and kissed him.

Jennifer was thanking him for more than his last words and they all knew it and the part he had played in getting his sister and her beloved together.

The music had turned soft and dreamy as they returned to the dance floor after the buffet. Already, couples were starting to take their leave, Carter's parents having left just after Jennifer and Adam.

Liberty didn't want the magic to stop. With morning would come the return into the real world. All she wanted now was his arms around her, his kisses, the magical feeling that they were in a place where thought and reason didn't exist.

They were almost the last to leave at two in the morning. The band had long since departed, just a lone piano player continuing to play for the couples smooching on the dance floor.

Liberty saw Carter tip him handsomely as she collected

her bag from the table. Then Carter joined her, his jacket slung over his arm as he hugged her to his side as they walked out of the room towards the lifts. 'Enjoyed it?' he asked smokily as they stepped into the little box. Then, as the doors glided shut, he didn't wait for an answer, taking her into his arms and kissing her until there was only Carter in all the universe. 'You taste sweet,' he murmured, 'like honey.'

'It's more likely to be champagne,' she whispered dreamily just as the doors opened at their floor. The corridor was absolutely silent, their footsteps muffled by the thick carpeting as they walked to Liberty's door.

'It's been a special evening.'

He smiled at her as he spoke and she thought how good he was not to harbour even a shred of resentment over the bracelet. She lifted her hand and touched his hard face, which was already slightly prickly under her fingers although she knew he'd been freshly shaved when he came to her room earlier. He was an incredibly virile man; even his beard grew twice as quickly as anyone else's. 'Carter,' she whispered, 'please kiss me.'

He put his mouth to hers, lightly stroking her lips open before he plunged swiftly into the undefended territory with his tongue, fuelling the wild surge of sensation that exploded inside her with consummate ease. His thighs were hard against hers as she clung to him, her body welcoming his touch as he stroked her breasts over the soft fine silk of her gown, teasing her nipples into hard peaks with the soft pads of his thumbs.

He made a harsh sound in his throat, and she was only half-aware of his hands moving over her shoulders, of the search for the key to open the dress at the nape of her neck. 'It hasn't got a zip.' Her voice was breathless as she came up for air. 'It goes over my head.'

He was breathing hard, and it was a moment before he said, 'Even your clothes conspire against me.'

The exchange had been enough to break the spiralling desire and, as he took a step backwards from her saying, 'Sleep well, Aphrodite,' Liberty didn't know if she wanted to laugh or cry.

In the event she did neither. 'Thank you for a lovely evening, Carter. And…and I'm sorry about the bracelet.'

He acknowledged the words with a twist to his mouth and a little salute, before turning as she put her key in the lock and stepped into the room.

Liberty had shut the door and taken several steps towards the bed before she realised it was occupied. Adam was laying fully dressed and sound asleep on the top of the covers, Jennifer being nothing more than a snuggled mound under the duvet in her own bed. Jennifer's dress was lying on the chair by the bed but there was no sign of her underwear. He had obviously helped her off with her dress before collapsing on the other bed, Liberty thought indulgently, walking across to him and taking him by the shoulder as she whispered, 'Adam? Adam, wake up.'

There was absolutely no response apart from a most unromantic snore. She tried again, and then again, her efforts becoming louder and more violent as he slept through them all. After she had all but bellowed in his ear, Liberty accepted defeat, standing back and glaring down at him.

Great. Just great. Tolerance and understanding had long since flown out of the window. What was she going to do now?

The answer came by a cautious knock at her door. When she opened it, Carter said, 'I seem to be missing a groom.'

'He's here.' Liberty flung the door wide and her voice was not quiet. 'In *my* bed. And he's not budging.'

'On it,' Carter corrected, grinning.

'Whatever.' She glared at him as though it was his fault. 'And I can't wake him.'

'You won't.' Carter was complacent. 'When he's like this he'll sleep through anything. When we were eighteen a bunch of us on a boating holiday tied up on a jetty near here on the Broads at high tide. We'd visited a few pubs that evening—' his tone suggested it was more than a few '—and we didn't allow any slack in the ropes. The tide went down and the boat was held at an angle of thirty degrees out of the water. Things were sliding and crashing, and Adam finished up out of his bed sleeping halfway up the wall. He slept through it all. Never knew a thing about it.'

Liberty eyed him grimly. 'Is that supposed to be helpful?'

'I'm just telling it how it was.'

She sent him a quick but lethal glance before looking towards the bed again. 'Can't you carry him to your room?' she asked plaintively. 'A fireman's lift or something?'

Yes, he could. But he wasn't going to get another opportunity like this one. It was gift-wrapped. 'Hardly,' he murmured reproachfully. 'He's a big lad at six foot two, and he'll be a dead weight the way he is now.'

She hadn't stamped her foot since she was a child but she stamped it now. 'Where do I sleep? In the bath?'

'Of course not.' He sounded shocked. 'There's a spare bed in my room, isn't there? Perfect solution.'

For whom? She stared at him. 'I don't think so.'

'Why ever not?' He was all innocence and reason.

'Because…' She didn't know quite how to put it into words and finished up staring at him somewhat helplessly.

'Liberty, we're two adult people,' he said patiently. 'The beds in this room are occupied and will stay that way till morning. The beds in my room are vacant. One for you and one for me. What could be more obvious?'

Put like that, nothing, but then Carter was in the equation.

'Of course, if you can't trust yourself not to keep your hands off me,' he said sadly, 'I understand.'

Arrogant swine. It was perfectly true, as it happened— she *didn't* trust herself, but he was still an arrogant swine for suggesting it, even if it was said tongue in cheek.

'Not at all,' she said with cold dignity.

'Well, then?' He smiled at her, a very normal, almost big brother type of smile. 'Problem solved, surely? You just bring what you need for the night and we'll let these two sleep it off. They have had a very big day,' he added fondly, almost as though she was the wicked despot in objecting to her bed being taken in the first place.

Liberty found herself between the devil and the deep blue sea. She couldn't sleep on the floor or in the bath, but there were far too many alarm bells ringing for comfort.

'Liberty?' He was looking at her as though she was crazy not to fall in with his suggestion. Maybe she was. Her brain was racing, and she couldn't see the wood for the trees.

'Okay,' she said at last. 'I'll get my night things.'

She was faintly reassured by the casual way he said, 'Fine. Come along when you're ready and don't forget to bring your key so you can get back in here in the morning.'

Carter's exit at this point was strategic and he admitted it to himself as he walked along the corridor to his own room, leaving the door ajar so Liberty could walk in. She was blocking him in every way, refusing to even try to escape the tight strangehold her mother had put on her emotions and ability to trust and love and feel.

He knew if he had her in his bed he could take her heavenwards. When he kissed her she melted like wax in his arms. At those times there was only truth between them, and the truth was that she wanted him every bit as much as he wanted her. Damn it, he wasn't asking for sex and sex alone. He wanted commitment, he'd told her that, and everything that went in the bag with it. Maybe it was time to rethink his strategy?

Every time he thought they'd made a step forward over the last weeks, there had been another step backwards. Her defences were so strong it could take years for her to trust him. And he didn't want to wait years. He didn't think he could stand it. She was forcing him to use the weapon against which she had no defence. Sex. The solution to their problem had been handed to him on a plate tonight and he wasn't going to let the opportunity go unheeded. He loved her, for crying out loud. What more did she want?

Liberty's heart was hammering painfully as she knocked on the half-open door of Carter's room. When there was no answer she peered round the door, only to find the bedroom empty. He must be in the bathroom.

She walked in tentatively, literally on tiptoe, and then, as she heard the unmistakable sound of the shower, she relaxed slightly, glancing nervously round the room.

It was clear which bed was Carter's. His evening jacket and trousers were slung across the cover in typical male disregard, the cover rumpled as though he had sat on it to remove his socks and shoes. Which he might have.

Liberty found her hand was at her throat and she forced

herself to walk across to the other bed as though this was a perfectly ordinary night. She sat on the very edge of the bed clutching her nightie, robe and shower bag to her chest, before she forced herself to relax her fingers and lay the clothes across her lap.

The sounds from the bathroom ceased and every muscle in her body tightened.

'Hi there.' Carter's voice was casual as he strolled into the bedroom, a towel wrapped low around his lean hips and his thickly muscled torso gleaming like oiled silk. 'I didn't hear you come in.'

'You were in the shower,' Liberty said faintly.

'Right.' He nodded, his eyes narrowing as they watched her. 'I thought I'd go in first and leave the way clear for you when you came along.'

She found it impossible to respond with any naturalness with the sight of acres and acres of bare male flesh in front of her, merely bobbing her head in the fashion of the toy dogs seen in the backs of cars. Did he sleep naked? It appeared so. She didn't think she could handle this situation.

'So if you want to go in now?' he pressed, waving his hand towards the *en suite* bathroom as she continued to sit like a fascinated rabbit in front of the snake about to devour it.

'Thank you.' She shot to her feet, dropping her nightie onto the floor and then whisking it up and almost falling over in the process. She regained her balance without looking at Carter again, disappearing into the bathroom and shutting the door. Should she lock it? She gazed at the door as though it was going to answer her. If she did it would look as though she didn't trust him not to behave like the worse peeping Tom; if she didn't he might assume she was offering an invitation for him to join her.

Her peace of mind overrode any consideration of Carter's feelings, and once she had locked the door she leant against it, weak-kneed. It took a minute or two for her heartbeat to return to normal, but once it had she asked herself why she was reacting like this anyway. Hadn't she been thinking that sleeping with him might sort out a few issues one way or the other? Maybe she should look on this as an act of fate? But she wasn't *ready*. The last word was a groan. It was all very well to imagine sleeping with Carter in the cold light of day, but quite different when the actual reality presented itself.

Take a shower. Undress and take a shower and behave normally. She grabbed at the mundane, pulling the dress over her head with scant regard for its fragility and cost and quickly divesting herself of her bra and panties. Once in the shower she tried to relax but found her nerves were as taut as piano wire, and the warm water flowing over her limbs didn't help one bit. She was just as tense when she'd finished.

After wrapping a bath sheet round her, she opened her shower bag and brought out her cleanser and eye make-up removing pads. The nightly routine helped a little and once her face was scrubbed clean she donned her nightie, looking at her squeaky-clean reflection in the mirror.

Maybe he would be asleep when she went into the bedroom? The thought mocked her. This was Carter. There was no way he would be asleep; neither would he pretend to be in aid of her modesty. It wasn't his style.

He didn't. 'I thought you might like a glass of water?' He was crouching by the little fridge in the room as she entered, the towel having been replaced by black silk pyjama bottoms. It should have been an improvement but the overall impact was so sensational it wasn't.

Liberty stared; she couldn't help it. The flagrant masculinity was too fascinating. The hair on his muscled chest narrowed to a thin line which disappeared into the pyjamas and his arms looked hard and powerful. He was lean and tanned and there wasn't an ounce of surplus flesh on him.

She licked her dry lips and saw the silver-grey eyes follow the movement. 'Th…thank you.'

'Sparkling or still?' he said offhandedly.

'What?' She heard the words but somehow they didn't register.

'The water,' he said patiently. 'Sparkling or still?'

'Oh, still, please.' She hoped she didn't scramble into bed but it felt like it.

'They're going to feel pretty embarrassed when they wake up in the morning.' He straightened, two bottles of water in his hands. 'Or Adam is at least, taking your bed like that.'

'What?' Oh, stop saying what, for goodness' sake, she told herself scathingly. You sound like the worst sort of imbecile.

'Adam and Jen.' He moved with animal grace, she noted, something catlike in the easy stride of his body. 'I'll get you a glass.' He placed the bottle of water on her bedside cabinet before disappearing into the bathroom for two glasses. She swallowed hard. Get a grip, Libby, she told herself faintly.

The main overhead light had already been off when she had entered the bedroom, a warm glow from a small table lamp in the corner of the room the only illumination. Hopefully the mellow light was flattering, she thought suddenly, and when that other section of her mind asked if it was important, she answered sharply in the affirmative. She wanted to look desirable to him, she wanted— Oh, she didn't know what she wanted. And then Carter walked out of the bathroom and she did. And how.

'How is it you look more beautiful fresh out of the shower without any paint on your face?' he asked softly. 'How do you do that?'

She looked at him, at the deep, dark glitter in his eyes and she knew what he wanted. She wanted it too. 'Do I?' she answered just as softly.

'Ravishingly so.' He placed the glass beside the bottle and then sat down on the edge of her bed. 'Do you know how much I want you?' he murmured. 'Have you any idea?'

She didn't prevaricate. 'I think so,' she said huskily, 'if it's anything like I want you.'

It surprised him, she could tell, but then she couldn't blame him for being taken aback. He must think she played hot and cold, and perhaps she did, but not intentionally. Never that. She was as bemused as he was half the time.

The last thread of self-preservation reared its head, asking her what she was doing in giving herself to this man. It went against everything she had told herself since she had met him, but somehow, tonight, none of that mattered. She didn't want to be sensible and careful and logical. She wanted— She wanted Carter. Even if it was just this once.

'I feel I've known you from the beginning of time,' he whispered against her mouth as he bent his head. 'Crazy, isn't it? I feel you've always been a part of me.'

She made no answer because his lips had moved over hers in a delicate kiss that was starting a quiver deep inside. She reached out, wrapping her arms round his neck, relishing the clean scent of his skin and the firmness of the muscled flesh beneath her fingers.

For a while he simply kissed and stroked her, his hands roaming over her body in gentle, tender caresses which nevertheless evoked a whirlwind of sensation, heating her blood and causing the quiver to spread to a trembling in her limbs she couldn't control.

She had closed her eyes, the shadowed darkness adding to the feeling she was in a world she had never been to before, a world where sweet, sensuous pleasure was the master and she was a willing servant. Time had ceased to exist.

An urgency was growing inside her and it burnt up all her inhibitions and doubts. They could have this, she thought, for as long as it lasted, for as long as he wanted her. It wouldn't last, of course, it couldn't. Real life wasn't like that. And she wasn't going to fool herself or think in terms of marriage or anything like that. That was too much commitment, too much trust. And when it went wrong the ripples affected so many people that it was devastating. But just being together, maybe even living together, perhaps she could handle that? That way, when it finished, it was just a quiet decision between two grown-up people. And she would survive afterwards. People did, however broken up they felt.

At some point he had laid her back on the pillows, lying down beside her, propped on one elbow as his mouth and other hand continued their sensual exploration. Now, as she felt him gently peel back her nightdress, exposing the twin peaks of her breasts, she shuddered with mingled pleasure and apprehension, hoping she was beautiful to him, good enough for him. And then she couldn't believe the sensations he drew forth.

She opened her eyes, reaching up to him again as she said, 'I want you to make love to me. I want us to be together for as long as you want me.'

His mouth had been fierce and hungry just moments before but as she finished speaking he froze, lying very still for an endless moment. His eyes were the only living entity in the shadowed darkness of his face, their grey depths glittering and hot. Then, without warning, he rolled off the bed and stood to his feet, looking down at her with the strangest expression twisting his countenance.

'What is it?' She felt a bolt of fear. What had she said? What had she done? 'Carter, what's the matter?'

He said nothing for a second or two but she saw he was breathing hard and his body was betraying the extent of his desire. Then he backed to the other bed, sitting down as though he had to put some space between them.

'Carter?' she said again. 'What have I done?'

'I'm not going to let it happen like this.'

She stared at him, unable to take in that he had really stopped. Then she dragged the nightdress over her breasts, her eyes wretched and her face flaming. He didn't want her.

He waited until she had squirmed under the duvet and pulled it tight against her before he said, 'I thought I could do this but it isn't right, not with you. Not now.'

Her mouth was trembling but she was determined not to cry in front of him. 'I don't know what you mean.'

'I know, that's the trouble.' His voice came sharp and curt.

For the first time she saw the anger on his face and she shrank from it. 'All through that—' he gestured to the bed '—you were still holding out on me, weren't you? Oh, not physically, I don't mean that, but in your head, where it really matters. You just don't trust I'm being honest with you.'

'I… I wasn't.' She had to stop her teeth from chattering and it took enormous will, making her voice flat. 'I spoke the truth; I do want you. I—' she hesitated and then knew she had to say it now because she would never have the courage again '—I love you.'

'But you don't trust me. You don't trust that I'll be there for you come what may, that this is going to last a lifetime. You don't believe that, do you?'

'No one can possibly say that for sure,' she whispered desperately. 'No one. Not you, not Jennifer and Adam—'

'Yes, they can.' He stared at her unblinkingly. 'I knew it the moment I clapped eyes on you. I love you, damn it. I love you so much it's driving me crazy.'

'If you really felt like that you wouldn't have stopped,' she said brokenly, saying exactly what was in her heart without caring how it sounded.

'It's because I feel like that I stopped,' he said softly, 'you mixed up, crazy nutcase, you. I don't want an affair with you, Liberty, I never have. I've had enough of those to last me a lifetime and they were fine then because the women weren't you. I want to marry you, damn it. Do you understand? I want to know you are my wife and I am your husband, that we've promised to forsake all others for the rest of our lives. Old-fashioned words maybe, and I'd be the first to admit I never thought I was an old-fashioned guy, but I hadn't met you then. I want children—' he saw her recoil but he went on '—and everything that comes with married life. Togetherness, waking up beside each other for the next umpteen years, growing old together, watching our grandchildren play in the sunshine—'

'I can't do all that. I'm not that person.'

'The hell you're not.' His eyes flashed his anger. 'That's exactly who you are. I know, in here—' he touched his chest above his heart '—because I know you better than you know yourself.'

'You don't.' She shook her head, her hair covering her cheeks like a veil and hiding her face from him. 'We've only known each other five minutes—'

'Long enough for you to ask me to make love to you,' he said with deliberate brutality, knowing he was fighting for his life here. 'Tell me you've done that with some other man in the past. Tell me you've even been tempted to think of it with another guy.'

There was no answer and she didn't move.

'You can't because it wouldn't be true. You know me, Liberty. You know me as the other part of you. Your body recognised it but you won't allow your brain to acknowledge it.'

'My mother uses sex as a weapon.' The words were very flat but he still had the feeling they were being torn out of her from somewhere so deep inside that blood was flowing. 'She always has, all her life. She's broken hearts and wrecked families, and all she's had to do is to lift her little finger and make it clear she's willing and the next sucker would fall in line. I don't want that to happen to me.'

'Are you saying you don't want to be like her or you're worried someone like her will come along and ruin what we have?' he asked, trying to understand.

'Whichever, both. Oh, I don't know…' She wasn't expressing this very well and she had to make him see. Had to make him understand that she could never give him all he wanted.

'Your mother's messed up her own life and plenty of others, I accept that, but don't let her mess up yours.' His voice was inscrutable but she didn't raise her head to look at him. 'She's convinced you the only kind of intimacy that survives is a sexual one. You don't trust men to withstand a come-on and you don't trust yourself that what you feel can last.'

She didn't deny it; she couldn't.

'So where does your father fit in with this?' Carter asked quietly. 'With your own mouth you've declared he waited for this Joan for years and years, and to your knowledge he hasn't played around.'

Her father was special. She twisted in the bed, knowing if she said that it would be like pouring petrol on the flames of his anger.

He seemed to sense what she couldn't say. 'Okay, your father is your father,' he said wryly after a minute or two. 'Probably not the best example in the world. What about my dad, though? You only have to see him with my mother to know he thinks she is the best thing since sliced bread and they've always been like that, believe me.'

But she wasn't Mary Blake. Whatever Carter's mother had to keep her husband's devotion, it didn't follow that she had the same thing, did it? In fact, she was sure she didn't. If her own mother could choose to walk out on her and be content to see her rarely—and then mainly to pick fault and criticise—it didn't bode well for a future partner, surely?

Liberty recognised the inconsistency in that reasoning even as she thought it, but it was a head acknowledgement, not a heart one.

'So where do we go from here, Liberty?' Carter asked after a moment or two. 'I'm damned if I'll have a casual, open-ended relationship with you, not only because it's not what you need but because I'd end up tearing myself apart with jealousy every minute you were out of my sight.'

She did look up then. Under the anger and pain there had been a note of dry humour. 'I don't know,' she said shakily, her face damp from the tears she had been hiding.

'Do you want to finish it here? To walk away?'

'No.' She hadn't had to think about the answer.

'But it's all got to be on your terms, that's what you're saying. If I want any sort of future with you it will be one of no commitment, no trust and no possibility of marriage and children. Is that right?' He was going out on a limb here and he knew it, but he had to make her see how damn unreasonable she was being.

She swallowed, looking at him searchingly, but his face was giving nothing away and she couldn't see his eyes clearly in the dim light. She loved him so. She loved him more than she would have thought it possible to ever love anyone or anything. If she agreed with what he had just stated he might well tell her he wasn't falling in with her terms and they were finished. But she couldn't lie or promise she would marry him either.

She put her hand to her eyes, pressing at her eyeballs with her thumb and finger in an effort to clear her mind. She couldn't think clearly; her thoughts were churning about in such a way she couldn't get a grasp on anything. She wished everything was as clear as it had been before she had met him. She had known what she wanted then, had known how her life was going to progress. It had all been in order with no emotion clouding the framework of the years. Now her emotions were master of her thinking and paralysed her reasoning process.

And over it all was fear. Fear that she might lose him, fear that things would go wrong, fear he would ask more of her than she was capable of, fear his love would slowly begin to ebb and die. But the biggest fear, the real daddy of them all, was the dread that he might persuade her to forget everything and give him that inner core of herself. Then the last fragment of self-protection would be gone and she would become utterly vulnerable.

'I... I would be committed to you for as long as we stayed together,' she said quietly, knowing she was skirting the issue but unable to say anything else. 'I don't want an open-ended relationship any more than you do.'

'So it would be monogamous, this...being together

which isn't quite being together? Until, of course, one of us wants out?' he added with acidic softness. 'And what if neither of us wants out, ever? We miss out on family life, kids, grandchildren, the whole caboodle?'

Put like that it did sound crazy, but he was so clever with words and she felt so muddled and tired. 'I don't know,' she muttered helplessly. 'Don't you see? I don't *know*.'

There was absolute silence for a moment or two. 'Go to sleep, Liberty,' he said very quietly. 'It's late.'

Go to sleep? Was he mad? A short mirthless laugh escaped her. 'Funny, but I don't think I can,' she said weakly, watching him as he swung his legs into bed and turned on his side away from her.

'Try.'

It was mordant and he had clearly finished talking. Liberty plumped her pillows, bashing them with far more severity than was needed and feeling she wanted to shout and scream and cry. Go to sleep, he had said. As though they had been talking about colour charts or their favourite books or some such trivia. Men were a different species.

She lay in rigid silence in the bed for some minutes, willing herself not to move and even swallowing only when she had to. She was sure he was lying awake across the room and it was the only comfort she felt. After what was probably some fifteen minutes she became aware of steady breathing from across the way, and when this was accompanied by a definite little intake of breath followed by the tiniest snore, she faced the inescapable fact that the unfeeling so-and-so had gone to sleep.

How could he? The hot sting of tears wouldn't be denied any longer and she let them have free rein, surreptitiously wiping her face with the back of her hand after a while just in case his sleep was feigned. But it wasn't. As he mumbled something and then turned onto his back she felt like going across and thumping him.

After another ten minutes she got out of bed and turned off the lamp in the corner of the room, knowing she would never sleep while it was on. Then she had a drink of water, slid down in bed again and lay in tense wakefulness, going over and over everything that had been said until her head felt as if it was bursting.

After that came a period of numbness but she was still no nearer to drifting off when early morning light began to filter stealthily into the room. She opened her eyes, turning on her side to look across at Carter as dawn broke more fully.

He was sound asleep and lying on his stomach, the duvet down to his waist. His face was turned towards her, one of his hands cupping the side of his head and the other spread out palm down on his pillow. His black hair was rumpled, a lock falling across his forehead in a way that would never be allowed when he was awake. For a second she could see the boy in him.

She stared at him and then quietly slid out of bed, moving silently to his side. She studied him for a long time, a luxury not possible normally.

The rugged, slightly harsh face was softer in sleep, the firm mouth more relaxed, although his determined chin and aquiline nose gave up none of their severity. It was a strong face, a face which spoke of experience and life, and frighteningly attractive.

Her brows came together as she tried to rationalise how he had managed to become so important to her in such a short time. When she had first met him she had tried to tell herself that the attraction was purely physical, but within days she'd had to admit it was more than that. She was more drawn to this man than anyone else she had met in her life. He had taken her heart. In spite of all her efforts to hang on to it, he had taken her heart and made it his own. And the fact that he said he loved her, that he had actually spoken of marriage and roses round the door, should make her the happiest woman in the world, shouldn't it? So why didn't it?

He stirred slightly, the muscles in his powerful shoulders and back tensing and then relaxing again as the steady breathing resumed once more.

She couldn't live without him. She stared down at him for a minute more before dropping a kiss as light as thistledown on his lips and padding back to her own bed. But what if she couldn't live *with* him or he, her? What if they tore each other apart like some couples did, what—?

*Enough.* Aware that she had lost the semblance of peace she had felt when she'd stood looking down at him, she turned over on her side and shut her eyes. Enough thinking for now. She was utterly spent.

# CHAPTER NINE

WHEN Liberty awoke next it was to the realisation that cold white sunlight was flooding the bedroom and she was being shaken gently. She opened her sleepy eyes to see Carter's head just above hers. 'Good morning.' He dropped the lightest of kisses on her lips. 'Breakfast is served.'

'Carter?' And then it all came flooding back.

'It is—' he consulted the gold watch on one tanned wrist '—exactly eleven o'clock and we have to vacate the room shortly after twelve. I thought you might like breakfast in bed. Are you hungry?' he asked matter-of-factly as though this was ordinary.

She rubbed the sleep out of her eyes, struggling into a sitting position and gazing at him vacantly. He was dressed and shaved and horribly bright-eyed and bushy-tailed. She glanced at the tray in his hands. 'Where's your breakfast?' she asked weakly. 'Aren't you having anything?'

'I breakfasted with Jen and Adam a couple of hours ago,' he informed her smoothly. 'They've left now but send their love and Jen says she'll be in touch later in the week.'

'But I—' She glanced at the door and then back at him. Adam must have been in to get his things together; worse, Carter would have been able to observe her while she was asleep. She didn't count that she had done exactly that with him because it was different. 'You should have woken me,' she muttered. 'Whatever did Adam think?'

'You were in his bed, not mine,' Carter pointed out reasonably. 'So he probably thought I was losing my touch.'

She glared at him. 'You know what I mean.'

'You were perfectly decent buried under the covers,' he drawled lazily. 'In fact, the only part visible was a little pink nose and a cloud of hair.'

He made her sound like a hamster in its nest. 'They'll think I was so rude not saying goodbye.'

'They haven't got a leg to stand on in the good manners stakes,' Carter pointed out dryly, 'considering Adam crashed out on your bed. Anyway, who the hell cares what they think?'

Obviously not him. She became aware that he was looking her over very thoroughly, and raised a self-conscious hand to her ruffled hair. 'I look a mess,' she murmured.

'You look sensational.' He grinned at her. 'I've been longing to know what you look like first thing and now I know. Soft, rumpled and as sexy as hell.'

She preferred that to the hamster thing.

Carter stared at her and wondered how he was going to keep his hands off her until she gave in and accepted she was going to become Mrs Blake. He nodded at the tray in his hands. 'Toast and preserves, orange juice, eggs and bacon and croissants,' he said lazily. 'And I've ordered a pot of coffee for half past eleven before we leave. I suggest you tuck in unless you're planning to travel home in that bit of satin?' His eyes went to her somewhat revealing nightie. 'Mind, I've no objection,' he added consideringly, 'although there might be the odd lorry driver that loses control if he looks down on us.'

Her smile was guarded; she wasn't at all sure where he was coming from. Last night might never have happened from his attitude this morning. Or was this the cheerful, no hard feelings brush-off? Suddenly she wasn't at all hungry.

Whether something of what she was feeling showed on her face she wasn't sure, but after placing the tray on her knees and plumping the pillows behind her back, he sat down on the edge of the bed and said softly, 'Eat, wench, and don't start all that thinking again. It's too early in the day.' He reached for a piece of toast, biting into it as he grinned at her.

He wouldn't smile at her like that if he was going to dump her. She reached for the orange juice and took a sip. And he wasn't the kind of man to declare undying love at night and then something else in the morning. She should have known that. There was something probing at the back of her mind but she ignored it and concentrated on the excellent breakfast.

The coffee came when she was in the shower, and after she had dressed and quickly blow-dried her hair she sat and drank a cup, watching Carter who was reading the Sunday paper, his coffee by his side. He was frowning slightly as he read and it really wasn't the moment to feel such a flood of sexual desire that she could have leapt on him then and there.

The discovery of her own sensuality, which had been awakened over the last weeks, was still surprising to her and she couldn't say she was easy with it. She didn't know if her mother was highly sexed or whether she endured rather than enjoyed the desire she awoke so easily in men, but before she met Carter she would have sworn on oath she was rather a cold person sexually. Then again, before she had met him she had been *determined* to believe she had a very low sex drive, she admitted ruefully. She wanted to be the antithesis of her mother and subconsciously that had been a very clear distinction between them.

She shook her head at herself, reflecting wryly that Carter had hit the nail on the head when he'd called her a nutcase the night before.

'What?' said Carter softly. 'What are you thinking?'

She hadn't been aware that the grey eyes had lifted from the paper and were now trained on her face. She shrugged. 'Just that people would have thought I was mad if they'd seen me walk out of here in my dressing gown a little while ago and then return with my suitcase, still in my dressing gown, a minute later,' she said evasively.

He smiled. 'It made sense for you to shower and get ready in here. One room cleared for the maids.' She had a feeling he didn't give a hoot about the maids, and this was confirmed when he added, 'I like to see you doing your hair and titivating anyway.'

'Titivating?' She glared at him teasingly. 'I'll have you know I get ready in double, no, a *tenth* of the time it takes most women.'

'I wouldn't argue with that,' he said easily. As her face changed, he knew immediately what she was thinking. He put the paper down, walking across to her and pulling her to her feet. 'Liberty, I've never pretended to be a saint,' he said softly. 'And if you're thinking that I've done this before, brought a girlfriend to a hotel, then I hold up my hands and plead guilty. What I haven't done before is to book different rooms.' And when she would have spoken he put a finger to her mouth as he said, 'And I would have done that whether Jennifer was along for the trip or not, okay? Trust me.'

It was the one thing she couldn't do.

As her face spoke out the truth his own changed. 'My future wife and the mother of my children is as far removed from my bachelor days as chalk to cheese.' The steel she had heard once or twice before underlined the words. 'And that's how I see you. This is different. You're different. *We're* different. If all I wanted was a tumble in the hay, why do you think I stopped last night?'

Liberty averted her face. How could she tell him that the thought of those other women—beautiful, intelligent, successful women—were like a sword thrust straight into her heart. She had never had to cope with the painful effects of jealousy before and she found it overwhelming. He had so many memories, so many stunning women to compare her with…

'You're you, Liberty.' His voice was soft now, tender. 'I'm not perfect and neither are you. Hell, I couldn't live with a saint any more than the next man. You might not believe it right now, but no other woman can fit me like you do, and no other man is your perfect match. I want *you*, your warmth, your sense of humour, your crazy way of thinking, your insecurities, your love. All of it—good, bad and indifferent. Because that's my woman.'

She wanted to believe him. She wanted it so badly that it was a physical pain in her chest.

'I want the prim solicitor in the little neat suits, the gorgeous redhead in a dress that looks like it's been sewn on her, and definitely, *definitely* the woman who will wake up beside me every morning of my life with rumpled hair and brown eyes like velvet. Think about it, sweetheart. Dream about it until it's so firmly fixed in there—' he touched her forehead with a gentle finger '—that nothing and no one can take it away.'

'You make it sound so simple and easy,' she whispered.

'Then I'm sorry.'

She stared at him in surprise.

'Because I know it isn't, not for you. For me, easy as

falling off a log.' He smiled at her, a confident smile. 'But you'll get there.'

She looked at him doubtfully. Leaning forward, Carter kissed her firmly on the mouth. 'You'll get there, sweetheart,' he repeated quietly. 'Take it on faith. And I'll know when you're ready.'

'How?' She stared at him in surprise.

'Because I know you better than you know yourself.'

'I'm not sure if I like the idea of that,' she said with some emphasis. 'In fact, I definitely *don't* like it.'

'Tough.' The steel was back in his voice. 'Because it's a fact and one you'd better start getting used to.'

Now she repeated the words he had said to her the night before. 'So where do we go from here?'

'From here?' He let go of her, walking over to the chair where he had placed his jacket earlier. Picking up his case, he slung the jacket over it before reaching for her things. 'From here we go to London,' he said evenly. 'Okay?'

When Liberty looked back on the next few months with hindsight she viewed them as a kaleidoscope of constantly changing emotions and experiences.

She had introduced Carter to her father and Joan when they had got back from the weekend away and, as she might have expected, the two men got on famously. Almost too well. It made her feel odd that the two men in her life seemed to understand her better than she understood herself.

When her father and Joan had a Christmas wedding Carter had been there to hold her hand and say all the right things to cover any awkward moments when she felt suddenly—and ridiculously, she was the first to admit—bereft.

When she had paid her Christmas visit to her mother she had summoned all her courage and asked Carter if he would like to accompany her. She hadn't known what she'd expected with that one, but Carter had been charm itself with her mother whilst letting the older woman know exactly what she could get away with and what she couldn't. When they had left the overheated apartment and the restless, dissatisfied woman who inhabited it, it was the first time in Liberty's life that she hadn't felt like throwing herself under a bus after seeing her mother.

She had asked Carter what he thought of Miranda once they were walking along the street away from the apartment, and he had stopped, taking her in his arms. 'She's the woman who gave birth to you, so biologically she's your mother,' he said quietly. 'However, I see absolutely nothing of her in you at all.'

He hadn't needed to say anything more, and on subsequent visits she had watched in awe as he had dealt with the older woman with courtesy but firmness, refusing to let Miranda speak ill of Liberty's father when she attempted to do so, and making it clear he wouldn't tolerate any disrespect to Liberty either.

Liberty had been privy to the amazing—and intensely enjoyable—sight of watching her mother bite her tongue and mind her manners, and with the experience came the ability to take a step backwards and shrug off some of the gremlins which had attached themselves to her from childhood.

'Gerard always used to pander to her,' she said one day in late January, when Carter had refused to fall in with Miranda's suggestion that they join her 'little dinner party' the next week. 'In fact, I sometimes used to think he preferred her to me.'

'Not possible.' Carter had smiled at her, his voice dry. 'The man was most certainly a fool but not certifiable, surely?'

The weeks passed at an alarming speed. When she wasn't at work she was with Carter. He wined and dined her, took her to the theatre, opera and cinema, they ice-skated, visited art galleries and museums, as well as having quiet walks through London's parks or by the Thames. They talked like Liberty had never talked to anyone before, laughed, even cried when she related a particularly harrowing case involving a little boy of four she had taken on.

Jennifer's wedding was arranged for the first day of May and, as she had said, it was just for immediate family and a couple of close friends, a party of twelve in all with the bride and groom. Liberty was reconciled to the cream and blue bridesmaid's dress she was wearing, and she'd had fun going with Jennifer for the dresses. Jennifer had persuaded her to try on the odd bride's dress herself, which had been a weird experience, especially when one in particular had transformed her into a fairy tale bride and she'd had to fight back the tears.

'It'll be you and Carter next,' Jennifer said brightly, misunderstanding the emotion. 'You wait and see.'

Liberty forced a smile and passed the moment off, but when she was in bed that night she examined how she felt for the first time in weeks. She loved Carter—she hadn't believed it possible to care so much, she was consumed by it—but the thought of marriage still scared her to death. It was like the ultimate dare—you did it and it was bound to go wrong.

And he knew. She would catch him sometimes studying her, the grey eyes holding a peculiar light and his face blank, incomprehensible. At those times she knew he was waiting, but if she looked straight at him the strange look would be gone and he would be Carter again. But how long would he continue to wait for that which she couldn't give? she asked herself bleakly. How long would he wait, frustrated and unfulfilled both sexually as well as emotionally? She had made it clear once or twice since the weekend with his parents that she would live with him if that was what he wanted, sleep with him, be a wife in every respect except going through the final ultimate commitment of a marriage ceremony, but he had ignored her overtures. It was all or nothing as far as he was concerned; he was that sort of guy once he had made up his mind about something.

Their lovemaking frequently brought them both to the brink but Carter always pulled back, even when Liberty was trembling with the sensual vibrations quivering between them, her body on fire and her equilibrium shot to pieces.

She knew the strain the situation was putting on Carter too. She lived in dread that one day he would decide enough was enough and give her an ultimatum, but he never did. He loved her. Strange, a man like Carter who could have any female he set eyes on, but he did seem to love her…

Liberty glanced at him now as they sat in his parents' lounge drinking coffee after one of Mary's huge Sunday roasts. She loved coming to their home, aware she was drinking in the warmth and easy banter that characterised their visits like a fine wine. It always left her feeling more positive these days.

'Ready for that walk?' He pulled her, protesting, to her feet. The April day was fine and unseasonably warm and they'd promised themselves a walk on the beach before they went back to the city, but that was before she'd eaten to satiety.

It was just as Liberty was walking through to the hall to collect her coat that the back door flew open and the next door neighbour—a young woman whose husband worked away on an oil rig—burst into the house calling for Mary, a screaming toddler wrapped in a blood-sodden blanket in her arms. It appeared the child, a little boy, had been playing in the garden and had sliced his leg open on a piece of slate.

Carter had whisked mum and toddler into the back of his car with Liberty in the front before she could blink. He drove swiftly to the local hospital's casualty department, keeping up a calming conversation with the young mother, who was as panic-stricken as her offspring. Once they had arrived they were seen within minutes, but then had to wait a while for the wound to be cleaned and stitched. At first the little boy was all tears and whimpers but Carter began to jolly the child along, displaying a patience and understanding which amazed Liberty.

Dusk was falling by the time they drew up outside Carter's parents' home again, and now nothing would content the little boy but that Carter carry him into his own house and up to bed.

'You made a hit there.' It had taken three stories and a promise that Carter would call in next time he was up before the child had gone to sleep, and Liberty's tone was dry as they left.

'I like kids,' he said easily. 'They're like animals at that age; they sense if you're putting on an act or if you really care. And what you see is what you get with them too.'

'And yet you told me when we first met you'd never planned to get married and have a family,' she reminded him quietly, stopping just outside his parents' front door and looking up into his face in the shadowed night. 'You weren't looking for that.'

'I still liked kids.' He shrugged. 'I always have, but that didn't mean I wouldn't have been content to do the bachelor thing for ever. I guess you could say I was married to the job for the first part of my working life; I needed to be to make the business a success. Then I met you.' His eyes were grey pools, deep and unfathomable. 'And everything changed. Suddenly it didn't seem to be important to be a free agent.'

She thought again of how he had been with the little boy. He was a man who should have a quiverful of children. The thought hit her on the raw, and she didn't realise her voice was so aggressive as it sounded when she said, 'What if you'd met me when you were younger? When you were still so determined to put everything into your business and were enjoying playing the field? How would you have looked at us then?'

He stared at her for a moment, and his voice was silky with an underlying coolness when he spoke. 'What do you want me to say, Liberty? That things would still have been the same between us? That I would have been ready to settle down then? I can't say that because I don't know. Time and circumstances make us the people we are today.'

'So that means no.' She stared at him, her chin tilted up.

'It means I don't know,' he repeated evenly. 'I hope I would still have recognised the one diamond amid all the semi-precious stones, but youth is brash. I was desperate to succeed and carve a future for myself where I'd be beholden to no man for a roof over my head or food on the table, that much is for sure, and I've never hidden that from you. Neither have I hidden the fact that I was still playing the field, as you put it, when I met you and it palled overnight. I can't give you any cast-iron guarantees on ifs and maybes from years ago; what I can and do give is a guarantee on how I feel now and will continue to feel.'

She stared at him. 'I'm sorry for being scratchy,' she said miserably, putting out a hand and touching his arm.

Then the depth of his understanding amazed her when he said, 'It was the kid, wasn't it? Little Joe. Liberty, having a family doesn't always end in hurt and disillusionment. Millions of parents the world over bring up their children in secure, happy homes without a whiff of divorce.'

'I know that. I *do* know that but it's hard to accept when you haven't had it mirrored to you personally.'

'I can buy that.' He nodded. 'But sooner or later you have to step out of victim mode and decide what *you* want.'

'I've never thought of myself as a victim,' she shot back, stung by the word. 'Never.'

'No? Well, you could have fooled me.' He took no notice of her outrage, continuing, 'Your reasoning behind not marrying and having a family is at least partly because you don't want your kids to go through what you did. The answer to that is not denying yourself the chance to be a mother and wife, but to make damn sure you marry the right guy and find out what proper family life really is. And that doesn't mean you have to give up your career either, while we're on the subject. You could work as much or as little outside the home as you want once kids came.'

'And what if I couldn't have children? What then?'

'We'd cry a bit and probably rail against the gods and then get on with our life,' he answered calmly. 'I don't want you because I'm looking for you to be some sort of baby machine in the future, Liberty. Let's get that straight right now. If kids came they'd be a blessing. If they didn't, they didn't. What would matter is us. *Us*. We'd be there before the kids came and when they leave we'd still be there. You just enable them to make what they want of their own lives; you don't live your life as a couple through them.'

He had an answer for everything. She was still smarting over the victim thing and knew her voice was truculent when she said, 'It must be wonderful to be so wise.'

'Unquestionably,' he agreed complacently, quite unmoved by her antagonism. 'And rewarding, very rewarding, especially when I can set some poor misguided but very beautiful female on the right road.'

She stuck out her tongue at him and he shook his head sorrowfully. 'Men of great wisdom are rarely appreciated in their own lifetime.'

She would have said a rude word but as Mary chose that moment to open the front door Liberty contented herself with a scathing glance before she marched into the house. In truth she was glad the conversation had ended on a lighter note because it had shaken her more than she would have liked.

Later, after the drive home and once Carter had left after a last kiss goodnight, she poured herself a very large glass of red wine and sat down in her little sitting room. She needed to do some serious thinking and it was such that she definitely needed the glass of wine too.

She had always closed her mind to the prospect of children, always. It wasn't the thought of having them or loving them or being there for them. She remembered a girl she'd worked with once who had stated categorically that she would never give her body over as an incubating machine to get distorted and fat, and she'd been amazed a woman could view such a miraculous event in that way. She'd always thought pregnant women, with their big bellies and remote serenity, beautiful.

And she liked children—babies, toddlers, argumentative

eight- and nine-year-olds—she liked them all, and understood them. Oh yes, she understood them all right; she could still remember what it had felt like to be small and helpless in an adult world. Her childhood had been painful, probably due in part to her. Because she had been so devastated by her mother leaving them and because it had affected her so deeply, the other children had seemed to recognise this peculiarity about her and honed in on it as a weakness.

Of course, with adult eyes she'd recognised it was just the fact that it made her slightly different which had been the problem. Children in glasses or with braces, those with big ears or a big nose or whatever, they were all targets, and there must have been others being teased like she was, but she had been too wrapped up in her own misery to notice.

Because of this and the sensitivity it had engendered, she had always found that the children of friends and relatives seemed to take to her and find it easy to confide in her. She had heard some mothers, fathers too, talk about their offspring's 'little' problems with humorous indulgence, but she knew a friend refusing to play any more or being left out of a party was just as big a tragedy to a child as an adult losing their job or being unable to pay their bills.

She took several sips of the wine before stretching out her legs and sighing loudly.

So she had no problem with being pregnant or knowing she could cope with the child as it grew. It had been the thought that she might be responsible for bringing a little life into the world who would be let down by its father which had been the sting in the tail. She would always be there for her kids, she knew it. But as for a man… At least three of her mother's lovers had left their children and the family home. It happened all the time.

So she was right in what she had determined. Wasn't she? She stared round the bright, clean room as though it could provide an answer. And, that being the case, why did she feel so...disturbed after her conversation with Carter? *Had* she founded her adult life on principles and a mind-set which was wrong? Or if not exactly wrong, had she been guilty of leaving out the one common denominator which made all her reasoning invalid? That of love, real love between a man and a woman. The sort of love that Carter's parents had, that her father had for Joan, that Carter professed for her.

She finished the glass of wine and poured another, ignoring the fact that this meant two-thirds of the bottle had gone and she had to get up early for work in the morning.

And what of her love for him? She bent forward, running her fingers through her hair before rising to pace the room. Would she ever leave him of her own free will? The possibility was laughable. Could she imagine loving him for the rest of her life? A definite affirmative. Did the thought of making babies with him, of carrying Carter's child under her heart thrill her? So much so she felt weak-kneed at the thought. Did she trust him when he said he would never stop loving her? She halted abruptly, her stomach churning. Did she? *Did she?*

'Do I?' She wrapped her arms round her waist, clutching her stomach as she bent forward in agony of mind. The sixty-four million dollar question and it was never going to go away.

She was beginning to. Her caution mocked her, telling her to speak out the truth and be done with it. Yes, she did, she thought she did, but it was too scary to contemplate.

She began the pacing again between sips of red wine. Had he brainwashed her? She tried to bring all her training to bear and separate fact from fiction, reality from wishful thinking. It would get her off the hook if she could tell herself he had, but in all honesty he had not. He had challenged her, certainly, been a constant thorn in her flesh in some respects, and hadn't budged an inch on what he believed, but there had been no brainwashing. He had just been…Carter.

She wasn't ready for this. She plumped down on the sofa again. She needed time to get her head round it before she suggested to him that anything had changed.

She finished the glass of wine, taking the bottle, the glass and her night things downstairs. Once in the bath she stayed in the warm bubbles far longer than she'd intended, her mind so active it was positively running away with her.

It was one thing to admit to herself that she had come to a point where she believed she could trust Carter, quite another to tell him. Whilst she didn't say anything her world was still safe. She frowned, swishing the water with irritable hands. She was a coward. She shut her eyes, leaning back with her head resting on the edge of the bath. And she had never realised that about herself but it was true. She was a coward at heart.

How would she ever get the nerve to take this jump out into thin air and say she would marry him? She didn't think she could. She really, *really* didn't think she could. And yet they couldn't go on as they were. She knew it and he knew it. He wouldn't wait for ever, no man would, and she couldn't expect him to. It was totally unfair.

An impossible situation. She sat up in the bath, angry with herself, Carter and the whole wide world. Or perhaps it was that she was an impossible woman. Whatever, in spite of all she'd acknowledged in the last hour or so she didn't feel any nearer to anything being resolved.

She didn't deserve him. She stood up, swishing water all over the floor. He needed a beautiful, bright and uncomplicated thing who would worship the ground he walked on and give him a baby every year until he had enough for a football team.

She heaved an unsteady breath. What was she going to *do*? And Jennifer's wedding, which was going to be a trial however you looked at it, was just three weeks away.

# CHAPTER TEN

THE run-up to Jennifer and Adam's big day only convinced Liberty more and more that she would never have the nerve to go through with a wedding. Everything that gave Carter's sister pleasure—choosing the hymns, deciding on what flowers she wanted, telling the hotel where Carter had booked the reception what colour scheme she needed for the small room he had reserved for the wedding party—gave Liberty a churning stomach and a panicky feeling she couldn't dispel however much she tried. Even the simplest of register office marriages still required a certain amount of planning, and even that, she felt, would make her sick with nerves.

No other women seemed to be like this. Liberty glanced round the small London church where the ceremony would take place the next day. She and Carter, along with Jennifer, Adam, Carter's parents and Adam's mother—his father having long since been out of the picture—were attending the dress rehearsal, and even now Jennifer was fairly quivering with excitement. Mary had a positively beatific smile on her face, almost matched by Adam's mother's transparent joy, and even the two ladies who were busy fixing posies on the stone pillars of the old building were beaming and nodding as the rehearsal progressed. Everyone seemed beside themselves with happiness! Everyone except her, and perhaps Carter.

Liberty glanced at him under her eyelashes. The last week or so he hadn't been himself but she couldn't put a finger on what had changed. He was still as attentive as ever although she thought once or twice he had seemed a little preoccupied before telling herself she was imagining it. But something *was* different. She felt the sick fear rise up in her throat, the same feeling which had kept her awake until the early hours the night before. She couldn't lose him. She didn't know what she would do if he told her they were through.

Her hands were clenched tightly together, and as she felt Carter take the one next to him, smoothing out her fingers in the palm of his hand, she forced herself to smile and say lightly, 'Bridesmaid nerves. I thought someone ought to have the jitters because Jen is literally gagging to get up that aisle.'

'Indecently so,' he agreed softly.

'She's going to be a beautiful bride.' Liberty wanted to snatch her hand away because she knew it was as cold as ice despite all the heaters round the church and the warm temperature. He would think she was even more of a nutcase if just running through someone else's ceremony affected her so badly.

'Adam would think so if she turned up in sackcloth and ashes, and that's all that matters in the long run.'

'I guess so.' Her smile was more natural this time. 'It's very good of you to give them such a terrific present.' He had paid for everything to do with the wedding along with sending them somewhere hot for their honeymoon as his gift.

'She's my kid sister and he's my best friend,' Carter said quietly. 'His restaurant is only just beginning to get in the black and money's always burnt a hole in Jen's pocket. Besides, we've all been waiting over ten years for this,' he added wryly.

'There is that.' She grinned at him, but then as the vicar called them to say this was the part where they, as the two witnesses, would accompany the bride and groom to the room at the side of the church for the signing of the register, the smile slid from her face.

Another ten minutes and it was all over, and once outside the church solid sheets of rain greeted them.

'Oh, no.' Jennifer's face was tragic. 'This wasn't forecast. It's supposed to be sunny all weekend.'

'Never you mind, lovey.' Adam's mother patted her future daughter-in-law's arm. 'Better tonight than tomorrow morning, eh? It'll be sunshine and blue skies tomorrow, you mark my words. A perfect May day.'

When Liberty awoke very early the next morning, just as a pink-edged dawn was making way for weak sunlight, she thought Adam's mother must be prophetic. Within an hour the sky was as blue as cornflowers, fluffy white clouds sailing in harmony with a May sun which was growing steadily warmer with each hour that passed. A perfect May day indeed.

It had been arranged that a cab would pick her up at nine in the morning to take her to Carter's house where Jennifer was, the wedding being scheduled for midday. When there was a knock at the door at eight, she bounded upstairs from the kitchen reflecting it was just as well she'd been up since the crack of dawn. Still, minor hiccups always occurred at a wedding.

She opened the door expecting to see a cheery-faced cab driver in front of her, and her mouth fell open when Carter said, 'Good morning, Aphrodite.'

'Carter?' Her expression changed to one of alarm. 'What's wrong? Is Jen all right? What's happened?'

'Nothing's happened.' He waved a nonchalant hand, a calm gesture which was too calm and revealed how deliberate his air of relaxation was. 'Can I come in?'

She waved him through, shutting the door after him and then turning to say, 'What is it? I thought the cab was coming at nine to pick me up and bring me to your place.'

'Good. That's what I wanted you to think.'

She frowned. 'Excuse me?'

'Liberty, my own true love.' He took her hand, going down on one knee as he drew a tiny box out of his pocket. 'Will you marry me? Now? Today?'

It was a good job the solid front door was behind her because she leant against it, her knees almost buckling. 'I… I don't…'

'Understand?' His smile was sweet but she saw something else which could have been uncertainty. 'It's simple, darling. I want you to marry me and I know that's what you want too, but I don't think if we do it the traditional way I'm ever going to get you up the aisle. This way there is no time for you to panic and get knotted up with nerves and run out on me at the last minute. All you have to do is to say yes.'

He opened the little box to reveal the most exquisite antique ring garnished with pearls and rubies. It was the ring of her dreams, exactly what she would have chosen. She stared at him dumbstruck. This was unreal. It couldn't be happening.

'Your wedding dress and my suit are in the car outside, along with your veil, shoes, bouquet and everything you need. I'll help you dress and you can help me with my cravat. It's not the conventional way of doing things but what the hell, we were never going to be a conventional couple anyway.'

'But…' She couldn't get the words tumbling about in her head in any sort of recognisable form. 'I don't…'

'The dress and veil are the ones you fell in love with that day when you were shopping with Jen,' he said softly.

'The shoes and bouquet I chose. If you say yes now we stick together until I put the ring on your finger at midday, and then for the rest of our lives. Will you, Liberty? Will you marry me, love me, have my babies and grow old with me?'

It was suddenly so immensely simple. 'Yes,' she said.

The next half an hour was a blur of kissing and murmured words of love, but eventually Liberty surfaced enough to say, 'But Jen and Adam? This was their day, their marriage.'

'It still is.' Carter had acquired a grin which stretched from ear to ear. 'But later. It's been put back to later.'

'Oh, Carter.' Her hand went to her mouth. 'Do they mind?'

'Mind? They're beside themselves in case you don't say yes. Jen hasn't slept a wink all night and she's told me to tell you if she looks a wreck on her wedding day it's your fault.'

'But when, how...?'

He seemed to understand what she had difficulty voicing. 'When was the day after we'd been to my parents for Sunday lunch. You were different. You looked at me differently. And I knew.'

'Knew?' she said, puzzled. 'Knew what?'

'It was time,' he said softly. 'I also knew I had as much chance of doing the white wedding with all the trimmings as a snowball has in hell. So I had a word with Jen and Adam and then we all went to see the vicar. They get married at one o'clock, we have their spot at midday. A sort of marriage by proxy.' He grinned at her. 'But I didn't see any other way of managing it than getting them to act as substitutes last night. The vicar was all smiles once I agreed to give a hefty donation to the church roof, even though it means he has to miss his lunch because he's got another wedding at two.'

'But the paperwork and everything?'

'Dealt with.' Carter smiled. 'It's no use being rich if you can't pull strings for your own wedding day, is it?'

'I… I don't believe this is happening.'

'Believe it.' He pulled her into his arms, holding her so tightly she could hardly breathe. 'By this afternoon you will be Mrs Blake.'

'My dad?' She pulled away suddenly, eyes anxious.

'Standing by to give you away. And he's given me a list of everyone he thought you'd want to be there, so the small wedding reception has swelled somewhat. As soon as Jennifer caught whiff of that she provided another few dozen names too. The hotel is mightily pleased,' he added wryly. 'From a small room we now have the ballroom with champagne flowing for over two hundred, and a sit down meal as well as an evening buffet.'

'A real wedding.' She gazed at him, nerves hitting for the first time. 'Oh, Carter.' She reached out to him blindly.

'Toast and coffee.' He took her hand. 'I'm starving. You make us breakfast and I'll phone and tell everyone the eagle has landed and it's go, go, go.'

'Oh, Carter.' She fell against him for a moment and he held her tight again. It would be all right. She could do this.

It was as they were sitting eating beans on toast that Liberty asked tentatively, 'Did you tell my mother about this?'

'I'd have sooner announced it to the town crier,' he said dryly. Miranda was holidaying in Monaco with what looked like to be husband number six.

'She'll yell blue murder because Dad knows and she didn't.'

'That's fine.' He smiled calmly. 'There was no way she was going to be there upsetting you and taking pot shots at your father and Joan. I'll deal with her. I might point out that if it was a choice of attending your wedding or catching this poor guy she's netted I thought there was no contest. She'll see reason.'

Liberty stared at him. With anyone but Carter that would have been ridiculous, but she had a feeling her mother would be like a lamb with him. Amazing man. *Amazing man.*

'I never thought I'd be eating beans on toast with my wife-to-be on my wedding day,' Carter said thoughtfully. 'But it's great, isn't it?'

She smiled back at him, her heart in her eyes. 'Great,' she assured him softly. 'Everyone should do it.'

After breakfast Carter brought all the finery in from the car and soon her small living room was engulfed in swathes of silk, organza and the sweet smell of cream roses and freesias.

Liberty was entranced with her posy, which was tied with cream satin ribbons and lace. 'It's beautiful, Carter.' She held the flowers to her nose, drinking in the perfume. 'I love roses and freesias. They're my favourite flowers.'

'I know.' And then he took the posy out of her hands, laying it to one side as he drew a narrow oblong box out of his pocket. 'Will you wear it today?' he asked softly, opening the lid whereupon the diamond bracelet sparkled up at her.

She flung her arms round his neck. 'Of course. Thank you, thank you.' She smiled at him, her face glowing.

'And this to match?' he asked gently.

'Oh, Carter.' She took the second box he had produced like a magician with a rabbit. Inside was an exquisite diamond pendant with diamond studs.

'Thank you.' Her voice was tender as she raised a loving hand to his face. She had come to understand that it meant a lot to him to be able to give and she knew she had to accept it.

'Not one word of reproach?' he asked dryly but with a twinkle in his eyes. 'Not even a "you shouldn't have"?'

'Not one.' She dimpled at him. 'Not on our wedding day.'

They helped each other dress, Liberty in the gossamer-fine wedding gown with an embroidered organza bodice which made her waist look tiny, and Carter in top hat and tails. It was as Carter was fixing her veil in place—no easy job for his large hands—that Liberty suddenly said, 'It's unlucky for a groom to see the bride before the ceremony on the wedding day.'

For a moment the old gremlins had reared their ugly heads and Carter immediately pulled her into his arms, careless of the beautiful dress. 'We've done this our way,' he said softly. 'Okay? The right way for us. And we aren't reliant on luck. What we have can't be affected by anything or anyone if we don't let it be. And we won't.'

'We won't?' she said, clinging to him for a moment.

'You bet we won't. Trust me, I know about these things.'

'The wise one?' She smiled up at him, reassured.

'You've got it.'

He kept talking to her until the car he had ordered pulled up outside, not giving her a minute to dwell on the past.

'I do love you, you know.' She looked deep into his eyes as they pulled up outside the church. 'You know that, don't you?'

'I've always known that.' He managed to sound magnificently humble and typically arrogant, and he looked hard and sexy and tough.

Liberty wanted to eat him alive.

Her father opened the car door, beaming at her but with tears in his eyes as he told her how beautiful, how breathtakingly beautiful, she looked. Joan was standing with him, and the two women hugged before Carter gave Liberty's hand to the man who had been father and mother to her all her life.

'You'll hang on to her until she's beside me in there?' It was said half in jest but again Liberty caught something in Carter's eyes that brought a lump to her throat.

What she'd put this poor man through. And then she looked at the church and the photographer hurrying down the small path leading to the arched door, and she reflected that Carter knew her better than she knew herself as her stomach turned over with blind panic.

'Never fear.' Her father had taken her arm in a grip which would have done credit to a ten ton wrestler. 'You get in there, lad, and we'll get the show on the road.'

As she watched Carter walk up the path to the church, stopping briefly for the photographer before continuing on in—Joan scampering behind him—she reflected that Carter was absolutely right. This had to be one weird wedding by most people's standards, but a wonderful one. A smile touched her face and some of the panic receded. Yes, a wonderful one.

'Ready, love?' Her father was smiling at her and Liberty's smile widened. She had the two men she loved beside her on this day.

'I'm ready,' she said huskily, wondering how it was you cried when you were sad but also when you were incredibly, fantastically, crazily happy. And she was, she was.

The church was packed when they entered. As the organ struck up the vicar didn't look at all surprised when cheer-

ing and whoops and hollers came from all over his con-
gregation.

Carter must have explained things thoroughly, Liberty
thought as she fixed her eyes on him standing tall and
proud with his father beside him. He had asked his father
to be his best man? But then somehow that was perfect in
this family she was being welcomed into. Already Mary
was like the mother she had never had and Jennifer like a
sister.

As she walked slowly towards Carter, turning her head
now and again when someone reached out to her, she saw
Mrs Harris sitting with Joan and the two of them were
already weeping copiously. There were old friends, some
of her work colleagues, relations—she could hardly believe it. All these people had been in on the secret and
never once had she guessed a thing.

'Okay, Pumpkin?' her father whispered just before they
reached Carter, and she nodded, her throat too full to speak
as Carter turned round and she saw the love in his face.

He reached out to her, oblivious of the vicar who had
just begun his, 'We are gathered here today in the sight of
God…' and took her into his arms, kissing her long and
hard before taking her hand in a firm grip and turning to
face the front.

The service passed by in something of a dream, but then
when it was time to walk through to the vestry to sign the
register, Liberty saw Adam and Jennifer—the latter
dressed in all her wedding finery except for her veil—rise
to join them. 'I thought it'd be nice for them to be our
witnesses as we'll be theirs.' Carter grinned at her, his arm
round her waist.

'Oh, Jen.' As the other bride reached her, Liberty
hugged her sister-in-law tightly. 'I didn't think you were
here.'

'We slipped in at the back after you'd arrived,' Jen whispered. 'Didn't want to steal your thunder but I knew I wouldn't have time to change before we get married.' She grinned at Liberty, looking extremely like her big brother for a moment. 'Great this, isn't it? One to tell all our kids and grandkids!'

There was laughter and happy tears during the signing of the register, and then, once the men had provided hand-kerchiefs and the women had mopped their eyes, they all marched out of the church to the stirring music Jennifer had chosen.

There was just time for some photographs to be taken and then Mary fixed her daughter's veil and everyone piled back into the church. Jennifer had insisted she still wanted Liberty to be her bridesmaid, and so when the music began Liberty found herself walking down the aisle for the second time in as many hours. When Carter joined her in the front pew after discharging his best man duties it was clear the irony was not lost on him.

'You've gone from the sublime to the ridiculous, you do realise that, don't you?' he murmured out of the side of his mouth as they listened to the ceremony proceeding. 'From my not being able to get you to agree to one walk down the aisle for months, you've now had two.'

She had slipped her arm in his and now she squeezed it, her heart in her eyes as she whispered, 'Lucky, lucky me.'

The sun was still shining as brightly as ever when they all exited the church again, and after another set of photographs outside the building they all sped off to the hotel where the reception was being held and more photographs—joint ones this time—in its pretty flowered garden.

By now Liberty was feeling this was a dream she never

wanted to wake up from, and as the day progressed she found herself enjoying every minute. Everyone seemed tickled pink by the circumstances of what had been a double wedding of sorts, most of the females present confessing it was the most romantic thing they'd ever heard of for a man to go the lengths Carter had, and most of the men—after seeing Liberty—saying they could understand why he had.

Carter was like a dog with two tails and Adam was just as euphoric, the pair of them making everyone howl during their speeches at many of the jokes they directed at themselves regarding their difficulty at getting their respective wives to tie the knot.

All the in-laws seemed to be getting on extremely well—Liberty's father and Joan promising they would stay with Mary and Paul Blake for a holiday by the sea in the summer when Carter's parents pressed them, and Joan inviting Adam's mother to Sunday lunch the next day.

Liberty became aware she was sitting with a silly smile on her face as the sit down meal finished with coffee, and as she glanced at Jennifer on the other side of her she saw the same bliss reflected in her sister-in-law's face. She reached for Jennifer's hand, squeezing it as she said, 'Thanks for being so generous with your big day, Jen.'

'It's a pleasure.' Jennifer beamed back, a gurgle in her voice as she added, 'It's certainly different from my first wedding, anyway! That was all pomp and ceremony.'

'You and Adam will be fine.'

'I know that.' Jennifer leant towards her, her voice confiding now. 'And so will you and Carter. He's been a different man since he met you. Not that he wasn't great before,' she added hurriedly, in case Liberty thought it a criticism. 'He's always been the best brother in the world and I mean that. But before he met you his business and everything that went with it consumed him, you know? Now he seems to have it in perspective.'

Liberty smiled. 'Meeting each other has worked like that for both of us. There was plenty I had to get into perspective, too. Far more than your brother,' she added ruefully.

'Good job this hotel had two honeymoon suites, don't you think?' Jennifer giggled. 'Now that's one thing I wasn't about to share. Has Carter told you where you're going on honeymoon yet? He wouldn't tell any of us.'

Liberty shook her head. 'Just that we'll be away six weeks and it's somewhere where we'll know no one and no one will know us.' She sighed happily. It sounded like utter heaven.

'He absolutely adores you, you know.'

Liberty nodded. 'Yes, I know,' she said softly.

After the meal the four of them did their bride and groom duties, conversing with their guests and chatting and laughing with everyone, both brides on their respective husbands' arms.

When the music began and the two couples emerged on the dance floor for the first dance the clapping and cheering nearly brought the roof down, but Liberty was barely aware of it, wrapped in Carter's arms as she was.

Carter danced—as he did everything else—expertly, and she felt she was floating in his arms. The scent and feel of him was all around her and every movement of the hard male body against her soft curves caused her to melt into him, until she couldn't have said where she ended and Carter began. 'This is agony, holding you, knowing you are mine and yet having to stay here for one more minute,' he whispered against her cheek, his voice rueful. 'I have longed for you, dreamed of holding you in my arms like this, with every barrier down and nothing to hinder us, for so long. And now we are surrounded by all these faces. Why don't they all go home where they belong?'

She giggled, looking up into his face and seeing he was only half-joking. 'You've arranged the band,' she reminded him softly, 'not to mention the buffet at ten o'clock. No one is going to go before then.'

He groaned. 'I must have been mad.'

But eventually, after an evening which everyone professed to be one of the best they'd had, the buffet was served, the last few dances were danced and the guests began to take their leave. Mary and Paul Blake came up to Carter and his bride.

'I hope you will be as happy as Paul and I have been,' Carter's mother whispered in Liberty's ear as she hugged her new daughter-in-law goodnight. 'Carter is very like his father and they are both one-woman men. He might not always be the easiest person in the world to live with,' she added with a little smile, 'but I do know he will love you with all his heart and soul, and that's everything really, isn't it?'

Liberty nodded. 'Everything.'

They walked into reception with Carter's parents, and once the older couple had disappeared in the lift to the room which Carter had booked for them, Liberty turned to head back to the ballroom.

'Hey, where do you think you're going, Mrs Blake?' Carter caught hold of her, turning her into him as he said, 'This is our moment to escape and we're taking it. Jen and Adam are still in there; they can see the last few off if they want but we're going to bed.'

She didn't argue. His grey eyes were devouring her and she wanted so much to be alone with him too.

The honeymoon suite was luxuriously, if a trifle excessively, cream and gold throughout, the massive bathroom boasting a jacuzzi big enough to host a football team in its cavernous depths, but the huge, billowy dream of a bed was the pièce de résistance. Carter eyed it with unconcealed relish.

In spite of their urgency, however, they undressed each other slowly, savouring the moment with little kisses and caresses as they touched and tasted and stroked. A swiftly growing heat had seeped into every nerve and cell of her body, causing her to shudder as he gently peeled the last remaining item of clothing, her brief lace panties, from her, leaving her naked beneath his burning eyes.

Her hands were shaking as she finished undressing him, the strong, hard length of his body with its erect manhood alien but pleasing to her bemused eyes. He was beautiful, magnificent, and she pressed against him, searching for his lips, suddenly shy. She so wanted to please him, so wanted this night to be perfect.

'I'm going to spend the rest of my life making you happy,' he said huskily against her lips, his hands caressing the silky swell of her buttocks as he held her against him. And then his mouth closed over hers in a kiss of such hunger she found herself moaning in answer to the need it expressed.

Time lost all meaning as they stood locked together in the middle of the lush room, their hands and mouths urgent and a raging need to become fused as one overriding everything else. When he carried her across to the bed she was already moist for him, but this was to be no quick, lusty coupling. Instead he continued to please her with his mouth and his hands, bringing all his experience to bear as he stroked her burningly sensitised skin to higher and higher heights of ecstasy.

Liberty had long since lost the power of thought when at last his hands lifted her to him, knowing only that the need and fiery ache which was eating her alive needed sating. As his energy possessed her a brief sharp pain caused her breath to catch in her throat and immediately he became still. His body was rigid with restraint as he groaned, 'Am I hurting you? Do you want me to stop?'

'No, no.' Already she could feel her body adjusting to the hard fullness of him and the pain was gone, leaving nothing but a sweet, warm ache in its wake.

His lips breathed her name again as he began to move, slowly at first and then with increasing rhythm as she made no effort to hide the pleasure she was experiencing. Mindful that this was her first time, he tried to be gentle, but her little moans of passion and the way her body had welcomed him was like an explosive trigger he couldn't control.

By the time they ascended into the heaven he had created he had possessed her to the hilt, taking them from one peak of pleasure to the next in an ever increasing spiral of sensation.

They lay locked together when they came back to the real world, their legs entwined and their heartbeats as one. She found she couldn't move, her senses still so shattered by this other universe he had introduced her to that she was even beyond speech.

After a while he stirred, moving gently from her before he pulled her into his side, his arm holding her tightly against his animal warmth. 'Go to sleep, my love,' he murmured softly, 'and dream of me.'

She turned her head, gazing at the strong face she had once thought hard and ruthless and the tenderness in his eyes humbled her. 'I love you,' she murmured sleepily. And then she slept.

\* \* \*

The room was still wrapped in the shadows of night when Liberty awoke, the faint glow from the standard lamp in the adjoining sitting room area which they hadn't turned off before making love providing just enough light for a dull glow against her closed eyelids.

For a moment her mind was still vague, luxuriating only in the bodily sensations of comfort and warmth and security, and then her drowsiness vanished as she opened her eyes, turning her head on the pillow to see Carter watching her. 'Good morning, Aphrodite,' he said very softly, his grey eyes dark and glittering.

Ridiculously after all they had shared—or maybe because of it—her face flooded with colour. 'What time is it?' she murmured weakly.

'Five o'clock.' He moved slightly to place his mouth on hers in a leisurely kiss which set her toes tingling, his own need apparent as he moulded her against the length of him.

And then his black head lifted again and he settled back on the pillows, one hand continuing to stroke her full, aching breasts and the flat silk of her stomach as he whispered, 'Any regrets in the cold light of day?'

For a moment Liberty was almost inclined to treat his words lightly, to make a comment along the lines that it was hardly even day yet, let alone cold, but something in the waiting stillness of the dark face stopped her.

Incredible though it seemed, he needed reassurance, she thought wonderingly. Her strong, tough Carter, who ruled his small empire with a rod of iron and had a reputation ruthless enough to guarantee no one would be foolish enough to mess with him, needed reassurance.

'Only that we didn't do this sooner,' she said, her heart in her eyes. She slowly lifted a tender hand to stroke the black stubble on his hard face. 'I love you, Carter, so much.' And then she knew it was time for the last shred of self-preservation to be dealt with and it wasn't hard, the love blazing out of his eyes melting it away. 'I love you with all my heart and soul and mind and body. I love you so much it scares me to death because I will never be able to do without you, and if anything happened to you I wouldn't want to live.'

'Nothing will happen to me.' He gathered her fiercely to him, raining hot burning kisses on her eyes and brow and cheeks before taking her quivering mouth in a kiss which was a promise in itself.

'Nothing, okay?' he whispered after a minute or so. 'We're going to grow old together, you and I, Mrs Blake, but not before we live life to the uttermost. We'll travel, see faraway places and dance by a moonlit sea until dawn. We'll have babies, lots of fat, healthy babies and we'll watch them grow secure and strong in a family unit which will provide them with everything they need to be well-balanced, good human beings. There'll be laughter and tears because that's part of family life, but we'll see everything through together, whatever life has in store. And over it all will be the blanket of love, my darling. Love for each other, love for our children, for our grandchildren. Do you believe me?'

She smiled radiantly. 'Yes,' she said firmly. And as he took her in his arms again she met him kiss for kiss, embrace for embrace, love for love, as she would do for the rest of their lives.

MILLS & BOON®

*Live the emotion*

# His Boardroom Mistress

In February 2005 By Request brings
back three favourite novels by our
bestselling Mills & Boon authors:

The Husband Assignment
*by Helen Bianchin*
The Baby Verdict *by Cathy Williams*
The Bedroom Business *by Sandra Marton*

**Seduction from 9-5…
and after hours!**

**On sale 4th February 2005**

# 4 FREE

## BOOKS AND A SURPRISE GIFT!

We would like to take this opportunity to thank you for reading this Mills & Boon® book by offering you the chance to take FOUR more specially selected titles from the Modern Romance™ series absolutely FREE! We're also making this offer to introduce you to the benefits of the Reader Service™—

- ★ FREE home delivery
- ★ FREE gifts and competitions
- ★ FREE monthly Newsletter
- ★ Exclusive Reader Service offers
- ★ Books available before they're in the shops

Accepting these FREE books and gift places you under no obligation to buy, you may cancel at any time, even after receiving your free shipment. Simply complete your details below and return the entire page to the address below. You don't even need a stamp!

**YES!** Please send me 4 free Modern Romance books and a surprise gift. I understand that unless you hear from me, I will receive 6 superb new titles every month for just £2.69 each, postage and packing free. I am under no obligation to purchase any books and may cancel my subscription at any time. The free books and gift will be mine to keep in any case.

P5ZED

Ms/Mrs/Miss/Mr ............................................Initials ....................................

BLOCK CAPITALS PLEASE

Surname ............................................................................................................

Address ............................................................................................................

............................................................................................................................

............................................................Postcode...........................................

**Send this whole page to:**
**UK: FREEPOST CN81, Croydon, CR9 3WZ**